• PERIL IN THE DARK •

— B O O K 10 —

CRAIG HALLORAN

PROLOGUE

Finally, please leave a review of PERIL IN THE DARK - BOOK 10 when you finish. I've typed my fingers to the bone writing it and your reviews are a huge help!

PERIL IN THE DARK REVIEW LINK

Dragon Wars: Peril in the Dark - Book 10

By Craig Halloran

★★★★

Copyright © 2020 by Craig Halloran

Amazon Edition

TWO-TEN BOOK PRESS

PO Box 4215, Charleston, WV 25364

ISBN eBook: 978-1-946218-84-1

ISBN Paperback: 979-8-680351-91-8

ISBN Hardback: 978-1-946218-85-8

www.dragonwarsbooks.com

Publisher's Note

This book is a work of fiction. Names, characters, places, and incidents either are the product of the author's imagination or are used fictitiously, and any resemblance to actual persons, living or dead, events, or locales is entirely coincidental.

✳ Created with Vellum

1

BATRAM'S BARTERY AND ARCANIA

THE ARCANIA HADN'T CHANGED over the ten years since Grey Cloak had last set foot inside. White candles with golden flames illuminated the murky interior of the hovel. A chandelier of candles hung high overhead, corroding brass sconces held more, and others flickered on candle stands on a black mahogany countertop.

Grey Cloak set his eyes on the glass case and rested his hands on the tall counter. Inside the glass case, on crushed-velvet sheets, were gorgeous sparkling treasures worth a fortune. It held necklaces with pink pearls, earrings with rubies as big as his knuckles, and a rapier with a diamond-encrusted handguard. Ancient scrolls were bound and stacked in one corner, and a gold hand mirror that didn't show a reflection rested near them.

"Where does he get all of this?" Grey Cloak muttered. He lifted his eyes and scanned the quiet room. "Batram?"

His voice carried for a moment, echoing down the deep corridor of drawers and shelving behind the countertop. Large brass-handled mahogany drawers, each big enough to hold a large body, made up the bottom of the shelves. As the web-covered drawers stacked up toward the top, they became smaller, and they didn't stop until they reached the top of the old building. Spiders of all sorts crawled along the shelves and stretched webbing from one drawer to another.

Grey Cloak cupped one hand to the side of his face and called again, "Oh, Batram! You have a customer!" He eyed the boar-head rug. "Where's your boss?" It didn't bat an eye. "Look at me, talking to a rug." He gave a nervous laugh. "Glad no one is around to see how silly I am." He turned his attention behind the counter and jumped ten feet backward. "Oh my!"

"Welcome!" the rug said as he landed right on top of it. "Don't forget to wipe your feet!"

Batram stood behind the counter in his monstrous spider form. He had the head of a tarantula, stood over ten feet tall, and wore a red-and-white striped coat. Sticking out of his sleeves were eight spidery legs with sticky fingers on the ends. His eight eyes were bright green, and he had stringy blond hair hanging over half of his eyes. His lower set of hands drummed on the counter. *Tickety. Tickety. Tickety.*

Grey Cloak clutched his hand over his pounding heart. "Is this how you greet all of your customers?"

"No," Batram replied in a coarse voice, "only you."

"Why doesn't that surprise me?" He approached the counter and gazed at the towering monstrosity. Rubbing his fingernails on his cloak, he asked, "So, how have you been?"

Batram leaned his big body over the counter and said, "Look at me. I'm the picture of health."

Grey Cloak rolled his eyes. "If you say so. Regardless, it's good to see you. You're a hard man... er, whatever to find, and I've been seeking you for some time."

Batram gave a smile full of tiny sharp teeth. "Have you, now? And why would that be after these many, many years?"

"Well, it's only been ten years in your time. Not mine— it's only been a year or so for me."

Batram swept his oily locks away from his eyes with his top hand and said, "That's a very interesting bit of information. How can that be? Did you travel through time?"

"You know about that?" Grey Cloak asked with a look of surprise.

Batram instantly turned into the form of a halfling and stood on the counter. His hair was curly and almost white, and he still wore the striped coat with a yellow flower. With eyes as big as saucers, he asked in a warm, excited voice, "You really traveled through time? I thought you were dead or locked in a dungeon." He rubbed his dimpled chin. "I never imagined this. Interesting. How did you do it?"

As relieved as Grey Cloak was to see Batram back in halfling form, he said, "I don't have time to explain all of the details. I'm in a hurry."

Batram started smoking a black-horn pipe that appeared from out of nowhere. He tapped his foot and said, "And I'm in no hurry. Please, share your story. I have to know. Besides, you aren't going anywhere."

Grey Cloak looked behind him. The red door was gone, and so was the boar-head carpet. Batram had played the same trick on him the first time they met, but the door was black then, not red. "I'm trying to save the world, you know."

"All the reason to be more thorough." Batram eyed him with his big blue eyes, tapped his foot, huffed out a smoke ring, and said, "Out with it."

He sighed and spit out a brief version of his encounter with the underlings he'd summoned from another world using the Figurine of Heroes. He finished it off by saying, "And that's why I came here. I need to find the figurine. I hoped that you might have it."

Batram let out a rusty chuckle. "So you are the one that let those terrors loose. Hah!" He spewed out a stream of smoke that made the room misty. "I should thank you, I suppose. Thanks to you, my business has boomed. Why, I've had every mage, wizard, and sorcerer from one side of Gapoli to the other in here. There have been knights and the finest swordsmen, each of them looking for a weapon to destroy the underlings. They've given me everything they have to beat them, yet the underlings thrive. And now you think you can defeat them?"

"If I have the figurine, I can send them back."

"Ho-hah, so you think it will be so simple. They will see you coming from leagues away. Certainly, they have prepared for it." Batram chewed on the stem of his pipe. "Over the years, I've gathered bits and pieces of information. Wizards love to talk. The ones from the Wizard Watch, the ones that survived, have fled. Those underlings have killed all who cross them, and the ones they didn't kill now serve them." He gave a chilling cackle. "As if Black Frost weren't enough to deal with. Now he has two invincible henchmen who control the Wizard Watch."

"They aren't invincible," Grey Cloak said. "I know how to beat them. The figurine will send them back. One word, and they are gone. I need your help, Batram. That's why I've been looking for you. The figurine is bound to have turned back up over the past ten years."

"And what makes you think that the underlings don't have it? Or Black Frost, for that matter? Hmm?"

"I don't know if they have it or not. That's why I'm here

to ask you." He looked Batram dead in the eye. "Do you have it?"

Batram raised his bushy white eyebrows. "It is smart of you that this is the first place you would look. As you well know, I've acquired many rare antiquities over the centuries." He placed his arms behind his back and started to pace over the glass panes of the countertop. "I like you, Grey Cloak. I do. You are scrappy." He shrugged. "You are trouble too. After all, you are the one that unleashed this terror on our world."

"It sounds to me like you know where the figurine is."

Batram spun on his heel and locked his intense eyes on him. "I do know where it is. But..." He lifted a stubby finger. "That information will cost you... dearly."

2

THE WAY BATRAM finished his last sentence made the muscles in Grey Cloak's lower back bunch. The halfling was up to something. He was always up to something.

Grey Cloak played along. "So, you do know where it is?" He cast his stare into the shelves behind the little man. "Is it *here*?"

"That would be your wish, wouldn't it?" Batram wagged his finger at him. "I've dealt with my share of slippery tongues, and you would dupe me into revealing an answer without paying for it."

"So, the figurine is not here?" Grey Cloak asked, hoping to catch Batram twitching, glancing, or doing something revealing.

"Didn't I just tell you? I won't be duped!" Batram said. All of his facial features, except for his mouth, were gone.

But the disturbing image of the halfling continued to speak. "Do you really think that I'll reveal anything to you? Try to be so clever, Grey Cloak. It will cost you."

"Fine."

He reached into his inner pockets and fished out a small pouch of gold coins. He'd acquired a lot of treasure in his working days in Monarch City. He tossed the purse to the eyeless Batram, who deftly snatched it out of the air.

"How'd you do that?"

"Just because you can't see my eyes, it doesn't mean that I don't have them." Batram shook a coin into his chubby palm and bit down on it. "Gold is one of my favorite flavors. Now, what was your question?"

"Do you have the figurine here?"

"No."

Batram pitched the sack of coins toward the top drawers. A small drawer pushed its way through the loose webbing, and the purse dropped inside. A pair of tarantulas with red-and-white stripes on their backs shoved the drawer closed.

"Next question."

Frustrated, Grey Cloak asked, "Was the figurine here... recently?"

Batram flexed his fingers repeatedly. The rest of his features appeared on his face. "That will cost you."

Grey Cloak groaned and asked, "Don't you even care what is happening out there?" He flung his hand in the direction of where the door used to be. "With all of this, you could help."

"That's not my purpose. Your purpose is to figure it out."

Grey Cloak tapped his head on the counter and gritted his teeth. He couldn't spend the entire day bartering with Batram. The others would be waiting for him. "Fine." He placed another pouch of gold on the table. "Where is the Figurine of Heroes?"

Batram's belly jiggled when he laughed. "That pittance isn't going to retrieve the answer you seek." He hung his gaze on the Cloak of Legends. "I told you it would cost you dearly."

Grey Cloak clasped his cloak about his neck and stepped away from the counter. The cloak wasn't some ordinary garment. It was a part of him and had saved his life more than a few times already. Most recently, it had saved him from becoming a pile of ashes from Thunderbreath's fire. "You don't want this. It won't even work for anyone else. You said so yourself."

"It won't work for just anyone, but it will work for others of a rare breed such as you."

Grey Cloak smirked for a moment. Batram had answered a question without payment. It wasn't what he wanted to hear, but it was helpful.

Perhaps he is not as clever as he thinks he is.

He gave a Batram a pouty look and said, "I can't part

with this. I'll be defenseless. How can I fight the under-lings, then?"

"You have your friends, a dragon, wizardry—the list goes on. Don't try to fool me." Batram tapped his temple with his index finger. "You need to rely more on your wits than your weapons. Give it up. Make a sacrifice. No good thing comes without sacrifice."

Grey Cloak's mind started to race as he clasped the cloak tighter. Sweat built on his brow.

Maybe I don't need the figurine.

I can stop the underlings without it.

There is more than one way to skin a cat.

I'll take my chances.

He swallowed the lump building in his throat.

Why does Batram want the cloak so badly, anyway?

He wants everything—the cloak, the figurine. It's mine. Why should I give it all to him?

"You are thinking too hard about this. The answer should be easy if you want to save the world."

"Well, that's easy for you to say! You never even leave this shack!"

"Oh, that will cost you. And to think that I was going to be reasonable." He pointed at the red door, which had reappeared along with the boar-head rug. "Perhaps it's time that you shopped elsewhere."

Grey Cloak cast nervous looks between the door and Batram. "No, no, I apologize." He tried to smooth things over. "Can you blame me for being irritable after all I've been through? This cloak..." He smoothed the fabric with his palm. "And I have been through a lot together."

"And perhaps you can redeem it."

"Redeem?"

"Yes. After all, this is a bartery. You can buy back what you have lost. But..." He huffed out a ring of smoke. "As I said, it will take a sacrifice on your part."

An idea sprang to Grey Cloak's mind. "Wait, wait, wait!" He reached into his pockets and removed the dragon charm he'd acquired in the Burnt Hills of Sulter Slay. Shaped like a flat egg and as smooth as a river stone, the precious jewel twinkled in his palm with an orange inner fire. He lifted it before Batram's eyes. "I have this!"

Batram planted his fists on his hips and tossed his head back with laughter. Finally, he regained his composure, wiped a tear from the corner of his eye, and said, "And I have no use for that whatsoever."

3

GREY CLOAK'S jaw almost hit the floor, and his shoulders sagged. "Is this a jest? You can't use a dragon charm?"

Batram said flatly, "No. And why would I want one? So I can sell or trade it and have it tracked back to me and have Black Frost breathing down my neck? No, thank you."

"How can he track you down if you disappear all the time?"

"That's *my* problem." Batram puffed out a ring of smoke, but he seemed to be having a hard time keeping his eyes off the beautiful charm. "Uh, get that thing out of my face. We are dealing for the cloak, unless you have something better to offer."

"Better to offer? This is a dragon charm. Don't you get it? You can control a dragon with this."

"Some dragons but not all. It depends on the user. Again, it's a problem that I don't want to have."

Grey Cloak wasn't going to take no for an answer. "Surely there is someone that could use this charm, eh?" He smiled at Batram. "Worst case, you can hide it in your drawers. Keep it safe from trouble."

"My drawers are fine." Batram ambled to the end of his counter and grabbed an hourglass made from copper. It was a large object, half as tall as he was. He brought it over and placed it before Grey Cloak's eyes. "You're on the clock now."

Grey Cloak's eyes widened as he watched the sand at the top rapidly slide through the hourglass's neck and build up on the bottom. "That's a very fast hourglass."

"Yes, it is. Now, are we going to deal or not?"

"I'm thinking."

"You've had enough time for that. Once the last grain drops, you're out of my shop, and who knows—it might be another ten years before you come back."

Grey Cloak's fingers dug into his palms. Batram had him right where he wanted him. "Fine!" He slapped the dragon charm on the counter and said, "But I'm keeping everything in the pockets." He unloaded several bags of gold and silver coins and placed them on the counter. There were three figurines carved from black onyx he'd made and two potion vials with corks waxed on the top. He pulled a dagger and a sword free from the inner folds and stuck an emerald and a gold coin into his pants pocket.

"Oh my," Batram said, rubbing his chin and marveling. "What else does it do?"

"I lost track," Grey Cloak said, slapping down item after item. He pulled out a gold necklace with small emeralds, a stuffed mouse, a pair of scissors, a spool of string, two dove feathers, a figurine of Codd, and a small five-pound anvil. "That's Dyphestive's. And you will tell me everything about the figurine's whereabouts. Who has it

and what to expect? I want details," Grey Cloak continued. "Agreed?"

"Of course. I will tell you everything that I know."

"You'd better. No games." By the time he finished emptying the pockets, a small trove of treasure and trinkets had piled up on the counter. "And I need something to carry all of that in."

Batram waved a hand. A pack of tarantulas hauled a leather sack across the floor behind the counter, climbed up the side, left the sack, scurried away, and vanished.

"You're running out of time," Batram said. The hourglass was halfway drained.

Grey Cloak started shoveling his objects into the sack with his arm. He slowly peeled the cloak away from his body, and a chill fell over him and made his arms break out in goose bumps. He held the cloak out toward Batram's outstretched fingers but pulled it back. "No tricks."

"No tricks. That wouldn't be good for business."

Grey Cloak handed the garment over. The hourglass only had a quarter of the sand left in the top. "Out with it."

"Gladly. The Figurine of Heroes is guarded in the Ruins of Thannis, which lie below the Iron Hills. You can gain entrance where the Inland Sea's waters spill into Monarch City's Outer Ring."

"What guards the figurine?"

"Thannis was a wicked city swallowed up by its own evil. It is said that the undead still thrive there, waiting for warm flesh to cross the darkness to satisfy their ravenous hunger. It is a wicked place. The living don't belong there."

Only a fingertip's width of sand was left in the top of the hourglass.

"Who put the figurine down there?"

Batram rolled the cloak up in his arms and smiled as the last grain of sand fell. "You did."

The red door opened wide and bathed the room in daylight. The rug said, "Come back soon!"

A powerful wind lifted Grey Cloak from his feet and started to whisk him toward the door. In the nick of time, he grabbed the sack of his goods. As the unseen force pulled him toward the door, he caught a glimpse of Batram in spider-monster form, cuddling the cloak and waving at him.

"Batram, you liar!"

Batram shrugged and said, "Lies are often a matter of

interpretation. Good luck finding the figurine." He waved the right side of his strange arms and hands. "Bring me the Sword of Chaos, and I'll return your cloak to you. Bye-bye!"

Grey Cloak's body sailed through the door, and he skipped across the road and slammed hard into a water trough. He heard a door slam shut, and by the time he looked up, Batram's Bartery and Arcania had vacated the narrow alley.

He rose, ignored the early-morning onlookers, and headed down the street with only one thing to say. "Zooks."

4

SUNLIGHT PEEKED through the grey clouds, shedding light on the dewdrop-covered beds of wildflowers gathered alongside the muddy road. The morning fog lifted, revealing a clear path of small rises over one hundred yards out. The morning birds sang as they darted from bush to bush and streaked across the sky. The hooves of trotting horses made sucking sounds as they were pulled out of the mudholes.

Jakoby, a dark-skinned bear of a man, sat tall in his saddle, leading the way. His steady gaze remained fixed on the road ahead. Riding beside him was Reginald the Razor, a much younger man with short, tawny hair. He was dressed in black leather armor and wore his many blades like a suit of clothing.

Right behind them was Gorva, a young and strong

orcen woman with a build that could have been cast in iron. Beside her was Leena, wearing black robes trimmed with gold. Her long cherry-red hair bounced off her back. They set their eyes against the wind and didn't look around.

Dyphestive and Grey Cloak guarded the rear, keeping pace. Dyphestive's mule, Cliff, loaded with gear, trailed behind them.

Aside from the thunder of hooves splashing through the mudholes, the journey had been quiet. The company rode for hours at a steady pace, straight for Raven Cliff. They had done so on Grey Cloak's orders, but at the moment, Grey Cloak wasn't speaking. Since they'd departed Harbor Lake, he had been quiet.

"Where's your cloak?" Dyphestive asked for the third time that day.

"We'll talk later, I said!" Grey Cloak replied. His voice drew a backward glance from Gorva. "Nothing to see here. Keep riding."

"Well, aren't you edgy? Will you tell me what is going on? And I'm not taking no for an answer. Where is your cloak?"

Grey Cloak gave his brother a steely gaze. "Can't an elf brood and not be bothered?"

"No, I want to know what is bothering you. It affects us."

"Not as much as me!"

Dyphestive frowned. "It must be bad. I think you'd feel better if you talked about it."

"I don't need to be consoled. I need time to think."

"About what?" Dyphestive asked.

"I'll talk when I feel like it. In the meantime—"

Jakoby and Razor brought their horses to a stop at the top of the next rise. Their horses nickered, stamped their hooves, and whinnied.

"We have a situation," Jakoby stated in a strong voice.

Farther down the road was a covered bridge guarded by troops of lizard men.

Dyphestive leaned over his saddle and squinted. "What in the world are they doing?"

"It looks like they are barring passage across the river," Razor quickly retorted. He poked his finger in the air and counted out loud. "One, two, four, eight, twelve... we can take them."

Gorva sat up in her saddle. She'd discarded her tattered clothing for a more suitable suit of leather armor that showed off her sinewy frame. "I agree."

"What do you want to do, Grey?" Dyphestive asked.

Grey Cloak's nostrils flared. "Obviously, we should ride down there and kill them."

"Those are Black Guard banners flapping in the wind down there," Jakoby warned. "I can see the mountain and thunderbolts. We could slay them, but I doubt it will stop with them."

"He's being sarcastic," Dyphestive said. "Right, Grey?"

"Who can tell the truth from a lie?" Grey Cloak replied.

"Boy, aren't you in a cryptic mood."

"That's putting it mildly."

Razor pulled the reins of his horse, turning the beast to face them. "I'm all for turning lizard men into fancy boots but not if we aren't all in. What's it going to be? Are we going to go through them or around them? Certainly, we can cross farther down the river."

"We won't be crossing on horseback. That river is too fast and deep," Gorva said.

"Do you think they are looking for us?" Jakoby asked.

Razor pulled his sword from its scabbard. "Well, if they are, they aren't taking me without a taste of steel first. I've been a prisoner for ten years, and I'm not going back to the island."

"Will you put that away?" Jakoby pushed Razor's sword down. "The lizard men aren't blind. They can see us."

Grey Cloak's brow furrowed, and he had a spacey look in his grey eyes, like he wasn't listening.

Dyphestive nudged him in the shoulder with his fist. "Are you thinking?"

"Of course I'm thinking. I'm always thinking." Grey Cloak's cross look swept over the group. "For you and you and you and you."

"Not for me!" Gorva fired back.

Leena gave him a stern frown.

"Stay here. I'll return," Grey Cloak said as he led his horse toward the bridge.

"What are you going to do?" Dyphestive asked.

"I'll think of something."

Dyphestive scratched his head as he watched Grey Cloak trot his horse toward the troops of lizard men, who had gathered in front of the bridge with spears. "He'd *better* think of something."

"Our friend is in a sour mood," Jakoby said. "What do you think is eating him?"

Dyphestive shrugged. "I don't know. I've never seen him like this before. He's been very chipper of late."

"He's an elf. Elves are moody," Gorva said.

Everyone in the company gave Gorva a doubtful look.

"What?" she asked. "They are."

"Said the pot to the kettle," Razor replied.

At the base of the hill, where the road met the bridge, Grey Cloak was surrounded by half a dozen lizard men with spears pointed at him. He lifted his arms and locked his fingers behind his head.

"Horseshoes," Dyphestive uttered as the muscles in his jaws clenched. "I don't like this."

5

"IF WORSE COMES TO WORST, we can take them out," Razor suggested. His horse, a black stallion with a white spot above the nose, snorted. "See, my fella wants to get in on the fight too."

Grey Cloak's fingers remained behind his head as he talked to the lizard men. He nodded back toward the company.

"What's he saying?" Gorva asked.

"I don't know," Dyphestive answered.

"I can read lips," Razor said. "He says, 'If you don't let us pass, we are going turn Razor loose on you. He's not only the finest swordsman in the world but very handsome and charming too.'"

"You can't read his lips if you can't see them. You are making lies," Gorva said.

Razor chuckled. "You caught me, angel. But I wasn't lying about what I said."

"Huh, finest swordsman, my big behind," Jakoby said with a grunt.

"Come now, Jakoby. You're too big to be as quick as me. I'd poke you three times before you got a nick on me," Razor said.

Jakoby's broad shoulders bounced when he laughed. "Keep telling yourself that." He leaned forward and set his gaze on Grey Cloak. The lizard men crowding him brought their spears dangerously close to his skin. Jakoby's hand locked around the pommel of his sword. "They are about to skewer him. We need to ride."

Dyphestive pulled his long sword halfway out of its sheath, and he led his horse forward. "Everyone, be ready."

Grey Cloak dropped his hands, and the lizard men backed away. A purse was exchanged between him and one of the lizard men.

"Everyone, settle down," Dyphestive said.

The lizard man emptied coins from the leather purse. He said something to Grey Cloak, and Grey Cloak twisted around in his saddle and waved the company down the slope. Dyphestive took a breath and shoved his sword back into its sheath. "It looks like my brother has it all taken care of."

Razor returned his weapons to their scabbards and said, "That's a shame. I needed some exercise."

"Jakoby, lead the way," Dyphestive said. "And don't eyeball the lizard men. Keep your eyes down and go."

"Aye," Jakoby agreed. "We might want to put a hood over Razor."

"Even better—I'll slay them all blindfolded."

"Where did you find this one?" Gorva asked Dyphestive.

"He's a present from Tatiana."

"Present?" Razor lifted his shoulders and nodded. "Yes, I am a gift, aren't I?"

The company met up with Grey Cloak and the lizard men soldiers.

Grey Cloak did the talking. He had an irritated look on his face. "There is a toll. It seems that Dark Mountain's reach is expanding, and they are charging for passage at all of the bridges. Fortunately, I scraped up enough to pay the toll for all of us. You're welcome."

The lizard men sauntered through the company, eyeballing everything that they carried. All of them were strapping brutes, thick in muscle that bulged behind their scaly green-brown skin.

"These are fine horses," the lizard man that had taken Grey Cloak's coins said. He had a hiss in his voice when he spoke. "And your group carries well-crafted weapons. What is your business?"

Grey Cloak's jaw tightened. His steely gaze narrowed, and he muttered something under his breath.

"What was that?" the leader of the lizard men demanded.

"Get your claws off me!" Gorva warned.

"What happened?" Dyphestive asked.

Gorva growled at a lizard man soldier that hovered by her legs. "This one put his hand on my thigh!"

"Can't say I blame him," Razor remarked.

"Sergeant, what is this about? I've paid the toll," Grey Cloak said.

"That was before I had a better look at your crew." There was no hiding the greedy look building in the lizard man's eyes. "You have fine weapons and fine beasts. We'll take them. But you can keep the mule and the rest of your gear."

"That's outrageous!" Grey Cloak said.

"No, that is the privilege of being a Black Guard. You'd be wise to join us. Perhaps you might get your gear back." The lizard man gave a hissing chuckle and waved his arms at his soldiers.

The lizard men surrounded them with spears pointed toward their guts.

"Get your hands up!" the sergeant demanded.

"I told you we should have gone with my plan, but no, you didn't listen," Razor said mockingly.

Not a single member of Talon lifted a hand.

Dyphestive's fingertips tingled. Judging by the scowls growing on everyone's faces, he knew a fight was coming.

Not to mention the dark look in Grey Cloak's eyes, which were burning a hole in the sergeant.

If we fight them, we'll have the entire Black Guard coming after us. There has to be a better way to settle this.

He was used to Grey Cloak doing all the talking, but his brother was acting strangely, making him uneasy. He cleared his throat and said, "We are mercenaries who serve the Doom Riders. We are on a mission for them."

"The who?" the sergeant asked.

Horseshoes.

Dyphestive straightened his back and stuck to his story. He lowered his voice and didn't hide his deadly intent and summoned his darker side, Iron Bones. "Don't let your greed blind those beady yellow eyes of yours. Everyone knows who the Doom Riders are. They have slain and slaughtered from one side of the world to the other. I'll tell you what—you can have our gear and our horses, and when we arrive on foot at their camp, and they ask where all of our horses and gear went, I'll send them back here for you to answer."

The lizard men's yellow eyes blossomed in their sockets, and they exchanged nervous glances with one another.

Finally, the sergeant humbly corrected himself and said, "Oh, *those* Doom Riders."

He stepped out of the way, and his men moved along with him.

"Apologies. It's been a while. Give them my best." He

approached Dyphestive and gave him the purse of coins. "A thousand apologies. We never saw you." With a wave of his hand, he shouted at his troops guarding the bridge. "Get out of the way!" He bowed and added, "Dragon speed to all of you."

6

THE MOON NESTLED BEHIND thick clouds that blanketed the skies. Talon set up camp in the woodland, far from the road.

Razor lay on his back near a small campfire, rumbling with laughter. "Oh-ho-ho-ho! I'd never seen a lizard man's eyes turn so round as when you told that tale about the Doom Riders. I swear their tails curled underneath their legs." He elbowed Gorva. "Did you see that?"

"Don't do that," Gorva said.

He propped himself up on his elbows, and his laughter started to subside. "The big fella scared them. You about scared me, too, with that deadly look you gave them. Where'd you draw that up from?"

"I thought about how much I hated the Doom Riders, and I don't know—it surfaced," Dyphestive replied as he chewed a portion of dried meat. He was sitting on the ground with Leena at his right hip. He allowed himself a smile. "I did scare them, didn't I?"

"Scared the scales off of them," Jakoby said as he stoked the fire with a stick. "It was a good move. Well done. I thought we were going to be in a scrap."

"I hoped for it, but seeing you make them shiver was worth me missing out on some practice," Razor added. "You've got an ugly side. It's gritty. I like it."

Leena put her hand on his knee. As usual, she hadn't said a word and stared at the flames. They created shadows on the black arachnid-like tattoo on her face, giving it movement like a living thing. It wasn't a pleasant thing to see, and Dyphestive felt sorry for her.

On the other side of the fire, Grey Cloak squatted, rocking back and forth on his toes. He wore a new riding cloak but appeared to be shivering.

"Since we've all settled down for the day, I think it's high time you told us what is going on," Dyphestive said. He picked up a twig and tossed it at his brother. It hit him in the head. "Grey Cloak?"

"Huh?" Grey Cloak blinked. "What?"

"You tell *us* what. You looked like you were going to kill the lizard men back at the bridge. What has gotten into you?" Dyphestive asked.

"Are you cold? It feels cold."

"It's chilly but not unbearable," Razor commented. He scooted toward Gorva. "I'm getting warmer."

Gorva stood and moved across from Razor and sat by Grey Cloak.

"Where are you going?" Razor asked.

"Away from you before I kill you," she said.

With a playful grin, he said, "You know, most women find me irresistible."

"Include me in the camp that finds you detestable."

"Ouch, that hurt. Well, no roses for you." Razor lay back down and closed his eyes. "See you in the morning."

Gorva gave Grey Cloak a stiff shove and said, "Out with it, moody elf. What has happened to you? You have the look of a devil since you lost your little cloak."

Grey Cloak sighed. "I didn't lose it, and it's not little." He glanced at his brother. "I had a run-in with Batram."

"You gave him the cloak?"

"I didn't give it to him. I traded it for information," Grey Cloak replied.

"Who is Batram?" Gorva asked.

Grey Cloak scratched the smooth skin on his cheek and said, "Uh, that's hard to explain."

"He's a merchant that lives in a magical store and appears and disappears," Dyphestive said. He'd only been in Batram's Bartery and Arcania once, when he'd first gone to Raven Cliff, but he'd never forgotten the memorable trip. "Grey Cloak sees him more than I do."

Razor chuckled with his eyes closed. "A magical store—now I've heard it all."

"It's true. Anyway, I traded the Cloak of Legends for information about the Figurine of Heroes," Grey Cloak said as he tightened his cloak over his shoulders. "And I've regretted it ever since. I feel like I lost a part of me."

Gorva nodded. "Ah, the cloak had powers. It saved you from Thunderbreath's fire, didn't it?"

"That's not all it did. And without it, my skull aches," Grey Cloak replied.

Jakoby broke his stick and tossed it into the fire. "Well, what did Batram say about the Figurine of Heroes? Where is it?"

Grey Cloak eyed the campfire. "He said it's in a place called the Ruins of Thannis."

Razor sat up like he'd risen from the dead. "Say that again."

"The Ruins of Thannis."

"That's what I thought you said." Razor lay back down. "It's been nice knowing you, and thanks for the rescue, but I'm not going there. Ever."

Grey Cloak perked up and asked, "What do you know about it?"

"Yes, I've never heard of it," Dyphestive said.

"Me either," Gorva said.

"I'm not talking about. It's bad luck to talk about it."

Razor curled up. "I'm not going to be turned into a zombie."

Dyphestive noticed Jakoby's glassy stare and asked, "Do you know this place?"

Jakoby nodded. "I have. It's no secret. Thannis is a city filled with the undead buried ages ago. It was a flourishing city of great wealth that rivaled Monarch City. Perhaps it was greater. For centuries, men and women have made the trek into the bowels of the world to snatch its glory." His heavy stare swept over his audience. "Some survived, most didn't, and the ones that made it were never the same. They lost everything and went insane."

"Or became zombies that are dancing in the depths as we speak of them," Razor said. "Pipe it up, already."

"How in the world did the Figurine of Heroes wind up down there?" Dyphestive asked.

"That's where Batram's information becomes interesting," Grey Cloak said. "He told me that *I* put it there."

Dyphestive's jaw dropped. "But that's impossible."

Grey Cloak smirked and replied, "Is it?"

7

PRISONER ISLAND

THE RISING morning tide crashed against Thunderbreath's dead body. The island guardian's body had sunk a quarter way deep into the sand, and his spiked tail floated over the water when they passed. He was surrounded by men and women wearing the black suits of armor of the Riskers. Several dragons were among them.

Commander Dirklen stood in front of Thunderbreath's skull, staring down at the defeated beast. A man of remarkable good looks, he wore a black suit of plate-mail armor perfectly fashioned to fit his well-knit frame. His sun-bleached hair was blond and wavy, and he had the chiseled facial features of a Monarch. An ugly scar ran down the side of his left cheek. Black Frost had given him the scar as a painful reminder of his past failures.

"Look at his skull. It's caved in," Dirklen remarked as he

moved closer to the dragon and pointed. Slimy ooze drained out of the fist-sized earhole. He gave his twin sister, Magnolia, who stood nearby, a disgusted look. "What sort of weapon could have caused this sort of damage? Who used it?"

"That is what we are here to find out, isn't it, brother?" Armored like Dirklen, Magnolia was an athletically built beauty with curious playfulness lurking in her eyes. She touched the ugly scar on her right cheek. "Perhaps a giant hit it."

"There aren't any giants around here. If there were, Thunderbreath would have killed them." He rubbed his well-groomed beard. "Something else did this. We'd better find it fast. Moray!"

A Risker in black armor hoofed it over, sand kicking up behind his heels. Moray was a big fellow whose broad face looked like it had been stuffed into his dragon helm, and the rest of his body bulged beneath his armor plates as well. He saluted. "Yes, Commander Dirklen."

"I thought this island was a prison camp," Dirklen said.

"It is, Commander."

Dirklen scanned his surroundings and asked, "Then where are the prisoners?"

"Most of them are confined to Braykurz, the city on the other side of the island. The Ministers of Evil watch over them," Moray said.

Dirklen grabbed Moray by his shoulder armor and

pulled him toward the beach. "Then why don't you hop on your dragon, fly over there, and find out if they know anything?"

"Uh... er..." Moray saluted again. "Yes, Commander." He sloshed his way through the tide and headed to his middling dragon.

"And take two more Riskers with you!" Dirklen shouted.

There were eight Riskers in all, each on a middling dragon. Only Dirklen and Magnolia had grand dragons, which sat on the beach.

"I know a quicker way to find out what caused this," Magnolia said as she moved out of the tide and joined her brother.

He rolled his eyes and said, "Fine, let's hear it."

"I can use my wizardry on Thunderbreath, and we can see the last thing he saw." She gave an all-knowing grin. "Who better to tell us what happened than him?"

"Your practice of wizardry is more like witchcraft, but if it will save us time, do it." He bowed and swung his arms at the dead dragon. "The beast is yours to manipulate."

"Why, thank you, and you really need to stop talking to me like I'm your subordinate. You have enough people that don't like you. I don't think you need any more." She waded knee-deep into the surge and hovered over Thunderbreath's good eye. With a grunt, she grabbed his horn and tilted his head farther over. "Thanks for the help."

Dirklen crossed his arms and said, "I didn't want to disrespect you."

Magnolia lifted Thunderbreath's eyelid, revealing an orange eye that was as big as her head. She removed a small dagger from her belt, pulled the eyelid over the upper rim of the eye, and pinned it up with her dagger. Then she glanced over her shoulder and said, "Don't worry. It doesn't hurt. He's dead."

"Ha-ha," Dirklen said dryly. "You do know that he's Black Frost's brother. I'd be careful about not defiling him."

"Don't worry. I'll be ever mindful." She placed both of her hands over the dragon's eye, closed her eyes, and uttered unintelligible words.

The hairs on the nape of Dirklen's neck rose as he watched the golden locks of his sister's hair rise. Her hands began to brighten with rose-colored mystic energy. Thunderbreath's head started to move. Dirklen stepped back, his jaw dropping, as his hand fell to the pommel of his sword.

Magnolia spread her arms out wide, and she moved them as if she were gently and slowly conducting a symphony. Thunderbreath's head lifted clear out of the water and turned to face her. He stared into her eyes as if hypnotized.

She rested her hands on the horn of his nose and made her way around to his eye. In the sweeping, haunting words of a siren, she said, "Oh, great Thunderbreath, the marvelous creation that you are, show us the final moments of your life."

The dragon huffed out a blast of cold breath. His tail rose from the water and lashed up and down.

"Is he alive?" Dirklen asked.

"Of course not. He's not even undead, only a shell of himself. But he's a shell with memories. Come, join me and gaze into the dragon's eye."

Dirklen joined his sister and stared into Thunderbreath's eye. Small images of a battle taking place on the beach came to life. There were manticores and men, though none that he recognized until the dragon glared down at Grey Cloak and Dyphestive. "No, no, that's not possible! They are dead. Gone!"

A wide-eyed Magnolia leaned closer to the image and asked, "And they are still so young? How can that be?"

"Who cares how old they look? They can't still be alive!" He saw a runt dragon being chased and a war mace crash into Thunderbreath's face. The image died.

Dirklen beat the dragon's eye with his mailed fist, shouting, "No! No! No!"

8

RAVEN CLIFF

A DUO of Riskers soared over the steeply pitched roofs and towers of Raven Cliff, toward the sun, which was fading behind the distant hills.

"Skreee!"

Grey Cloak and Gorva entered the city on foot, leaving Dyphestive, Leena, Jakoby, and Razor on the northern outskirts of the once robust and cheerful town. Both of them donned traveling cloaks and kept their hoods up, shielding them from drizzling rain and prying eyes.

"Have you ever been here before?" Grey Cloak asked Gorva.

"When I was a girl, my family passed through here a few times to load up with supplies," she said as she stepped over a puddle in the messy cobblestone street. "This place was in much better shape back then, and the people didn't wear the long faces that we see now."

"Skreee!"

A dragon and its rider buzzed a bell tower fewer than two blocks away, circled, and landed on the tower's roof. It was a middling dragon, a dark-scaled beast with pitch-black wings. Its rider wore black plate armor and the open-faced helm of a Risker.

Grey Cloak caught Gorva staring at the Risker and said, "Keep your eyes off of them. Their sight is keener than you think. The last time I was here, I saw a woman and her child snatched from the ground for looking."

"What happened to them?"

"They were dropped off outside the city."

Gorva pulled her hood down and said, "That is evil. How can men be so evil?"

"Men? It was a woman Risker," he said.

"You know what I mean."

"Dark Mountain raises the Riskers to be cruel and merciless," he said as he picked his way through the citizens that were traveling home from another day of work. "The Riskers don't have parents to nurture and love them. When they are children, they are separated from all of that attention. They are taught that it makes them weak."

Gorva gave him a sad look. "And you were one of them?"

"Dyphestive and I both."

"How come you didn't become like them?"

He shrugged. "I guess they couldn't beat the good out of us. Heh. Not that I'm that good. If I had my way, I'd prefer to be doing something else. That's what got me into this mess in the first place."

A squad of Black Guard wearing crimson tunics with Dark Mountain's insignia over chain mail marched down the middle of the street toward them. The citizens scattered, and Grey Cloak pulled Gorva by the hand toward the open end of an alley and pressed her back against the wall.

"What are you doing?" she asked, twisting her wrist out of his grasp. "I know how to take care of myself."

The Black Guard marched by, and he said, "Sorry, I wasn't thinking."

She slapped him on the rump. "It's fine, elf. I'm only teasing you."

He smirked. "That's good, I think."

He took a step toward the street, and she pulled him back. "Tell me more about Dark Mountain."

"Now?"

"You seem to be feeling better, and I want to know more about you."

He rubbed his head. The truth was that he *was* feeling better. Even though he missed the Cloak of Legends, he'd begun to overcome his withdrawal from it and was starting to feel more like himself. "I was raised in Dark Mountain, and no one told me any different about right and wrong, but in my heart, I knew. Well, not exactly, but I didn't like not having any choice in my life. That... bothered me."

"And Dyphestive too?"

"He never talked about it. I did all the talking. I think since I was the only friend he had, he followed along with my plan." He raised his eyebrows. "I can't really explain his motivations. I don't understand them myself."

"He had faith in you, and you are his friend. He is loyal to you. What else is there to understand?"

"Why would anyone want a friend like me?" He flashed a grin. "I'll only get you into trouble."

Gorva offered him a smile and said, "I like trouble. Now tell me more about Zora and Tanlin."

He peeked around the corner and pointed. "Another street down is where Tanlin's Fine Fittings and Embroidery is located. I have no idea if he's still alive or not, but Zora went after him. They are a smart pair, but they are watched by the Black Guard and a yonder."

"A yonder?"

"It's a giant eyeball with wings. It keeps tabs on Tanlin and Zora."

"Why?"

"I think because they're still looking for Dyphestive and me. Anyway, the yonder keep to the back alleys. The Black Guard hovers in the streets near the front." He turned and pulled his hood down. "I think they know what to look for with me, but you, they haven't seen before. I'll be close by, but you are going to have to be the one to go and contact Tanlin and Zora. Be discreet." He placed a small purse of coins in her hand and gave her a wink and a goofy smile. "Buy yourself something real nice."

She stuffed the purse under her cloak and gave him a doubtful look. "And what if something goes amiss?"

"Then run like a bat out of the netherworld."

9

"CAN I HELP YOU?"

Gorva shook the rain off her cloak at the threshold of Tanlin's store and eyed him. As Grey Cloak had described, Tanlin was an older slender man with kinky hair, high cheekbones, and dark circles under his eyes. His white shirt was neatly pressed, as were his trousers. His warm smile and soothing voice were very welcoming.

She cleared her throat and said, "Yes."

"My name is Tanlin, the same as the name on the shop." He extended his hands and added, "Let me help you with your cloak."

She shed her cloak and handed it to him. While he hung the cloak up on a peg behind the door, her gaze swept over the room. The store was filled with neatly organized racks of hanging clothing. The outer walls were covered in box-shaped shelves filled with shirts and trousers.

Gorva sauntered deeper into the store, and her arms brushed against fancy and well-made dresses. She plucked one from its hanger. It was a long white gown with pearly beads embroidered into the chest and shoulders.

"Are you looking for something formal?" Tanlin asked. His hands were hidden behind his back, and he kept the same easy smile on his face.

"Uh, no," she said. "I was thinking about something for everyday wear."

Tanlin looked her up and down. "Please don't take offense, but your leather armor screams warrior. Would you like to switch to something more casual?"

"Maybe, but I like my leather armor."

"I see." Tanlin began plucking clothing from the racks. Among them were several tunic dresses. He held them up. "How about you try on one of these? They might be snug, as I don't have many customers with your strong build. No offense. There is a dressing room over there in the corner."

"Are there any other helpers that might give me an opinion? A woman, perhaps?" she asked.

Grey Cloak hadn't told her as much about Tanlin as he had Zora. He wanted Gorva to find out if both of them were alive. Streak had told them about Zora's run-in with the Scourge and how Tanlin was in danger. Since Zora had gone to rescue him, it seemed odd that Tanlin was doing fine.

Tanlin wagged a finger at her. "Ah, you want a second opinion. Well, that can be arranged." He clapped. "Zora!"

"Coming!" a woman hollered from the storeroom.

"Apologies." Tanlin gave a polite bow. "I don't keep as much help on hand on dreary days such as this. Business is slow."

A very pretty half-elf woman with short auburn hair appeared from behind the curtain that led into the back of the shop. Her green eyes widened when she caught sight of Gorva. Dressed in a white blouse and a blue skirt, the mildly obese woman hurried to Tanlin's side and asked, "What can I do to help?"

"Our friend would like your opinion on some more fashionable casual wear." He offered Zora the clothing he had draped over his arm. "I thought these would be a good start."

"Yeah, well, these might fit until she bends over to lace her boots and rips the back open." Zora giggled. "Sorry, but we don't have many gals with your burly build."

"I'm not burly," Gorva said. "I'm an orc."

"Don't be offended. We have plenty of clothing fit for orcs in the store and in the back. The truth is that we haven't been selling much at all lately, except to the Monarchs and the Black Guard families. They are the only ones with money to spend these days." Zora tossed the tunic dresses into Tanlin's awaiting arms. "Stay right here. I'll be back."

Gorva wasn't in the mood to try on dresses. Zora and Tanlin were there, and it was time to declare her intentions. "No, wait."

Zora stopped and turned. "Yes?"

A dripping-wet Black Guard entered the store. He was a big orc, taller and broader than Gorva, bald on top, with thick sideburns and a beard that were well trimmed. On the other side of the door and windows, more soldiers waited.

"Excuse me," Tanlin said as he spun on his heel and made a beeline for the Black Guard. "Sergeant Slot, how is life treating you today? I have your men's tunics ready."

Gorva noticed Zora stepping in front of her, shielding her from Sergeant Slot's watchful gaze. It didn't do any good. Sergeant Slot had already caught her eye. The corner of his lips turned up, and a hungry look built in his eyes. He shoved Tanlin away and approached Gorva and Zora.

"Who do we have here?" He took Gorva by the hand, brought it up to his lips, and kissed it. "I'm Sergeant Slot. Twenty seasons with the Black Guard. I'm honored to make your acquaintance."

"I bet you are." Gorva pulled her hand away. "I'm in the middle of something. Do you mind, Sergeant Slot?"

He seized her wrist and said, "Indeed, I do. You see, it's my job to get to know the people who come and go in my district. And I've never seen you before. I'm certain to have remembered a beauty like you." He gave her the once-over. "You are dressed like a warrior and carry a dagger."

"Would you expect anything less from an orc? Look around, Sergeant. I'm in a clothing shop, looking to dress down my attire. If you would do me a service, let me go about my business, and you can go about yours."

Sergeant Slot stuck his broad chin out, shook his head, and said, "I give the orders, not you. Tell me your name and where you come from."

"I'm Gorva from Portham," she said.

"And what brings you to Raven Cliff?"

"A feud between me and my... current mate?" she said.

"Ah." He gave a devilish grin. "Having a falling out, and you want to get away. I'll tell you what." He hooked her arm and led her toward the door. "My shift is over. Let me show you around Raven Cliff. It would be my pleasure."

She caught Tanlin and Zora's concerned looks. "That's not necessary."

"I'm not giving you a choice."

10

GORVA PULLED her arm away and said, "At least let me change into an outfit more pleasing to your eyes. After all, that is what I'm here for."

"I like what you have on," Sergeant Slot said.

"Please, I look like rabble in this."

He kissed her hand again. "I like rabble."

Gorva broke away from Sergeant Slot and said to Zora, "Come with me, girl. Find me something fetching, and find it quick." She practically shoved Zora behind the curtain. "Don't go anywhere, Sergeant Slot. I'll return shortly."

Sergeant Slot leaned one elbow on the counter and gave a smile as broad as a river. "I'm not going anywhere."

Gorva passed through the curtains and pushed Zora farther back into the storeroom.

"Easy!" Zora said.

She clamped her hand over Zora's mouth and pinned her against the wall. Then she felt a prick against her belly. Zora held a dagger against her stomach.

Keeping her voice low, Gorva said, "There is no need for that, Zora. I'm a friend. I'm with Grey Cloak."

Zora's eyes widened. She lowered her dagger and gently pulled Gorva's hand down from her mouth. "How do I know that?"

"When you see him for yourself."

"So, he escaped Prisoner Island?"

Gorva nodded. "All of us did."

"'All of us' who?"

"Dyphestive, Jakoby, Leena, and Razor. There were some others, but you don't know them."

Zora let out a relieved sigh. "I can't believe it. I was so worried."

"You didn't seem worried, as you are here, going about your business. I thought Tanlin was in danger."

"Don't worry. We handled the problem."

"Gorva!" Sergeant Slot hollered from the front of the store. "I don't like to be kept waiting. Don't make me come in there and shackle you."

"Be patient. I'm worth it!" She turned to Zora. "Find me something to wear quickly."

"You aren't really going to go with him, are you?" Zora rummaged through more outfits on the storeroom shelves.

"I can handle myself."

"Are you sure? Sergeant Slot is dangerous. They all are. This is not a safe place."

Gorva peeked through the curtain. Sergeant Slot was receiving a package of bundled tunics from Tanlin. Some of his soldiers had sauntered into the store. "I can see that, but don't worry about me. I can handle them. You need to rendezvous with Grey Cloak. Will that be a problem?"

"Me, finding Grey Cloak?" She tossed Gorva a crimson-and-gold tunic dress. "No problem."

Gorva was led out of Tanlin's Fine Fittings and Embroidery by a small host of Black Guard. Grey Cloak watched with big eyes from across the street.

No. No. No. No. No.

He moved out of the alley and took to the crowded porches, where many citizens were avoiding the rain. From a distance, he kept his feet moving and his eyes on Gorva. An orc Black Guard had his arm around her waist and hurried her along down the rain-slick streets.

How did this happen?

Grey Cloak caught several glimpses through the store window of Tanlin, who'd been addressing the Black Guard from behind the merchant counter. Grey Cloak's stomach had knotted when he saw the orc escort Gorva out of the building.

Traitor. It was the first word that came to mind when Gorva was hustled away by the soldiers. Obviously, Gorva had revealed herself to Tanlin, and Tanlin turned her in.

Everything is peachy in your life, isn't it, Tanlin?

He jumped off the end of a porch, crossed the alley, and leaped onto another porch, bumping into a portly man who staggered out of a tavern.

"Watch where you're going," the man slurred. He took a clumsy swing at Grey Cloak, lost his footing, teetered off the porch, and splashed into a water trough. He came up gasping.

"I think it's you that needs to watch where you're going," Grey Cloak muttered as he kept following Gorva.

The orc Black Guard stopped in the road and dismissed the other soldiers, who moved on.

Grey Cloak hid behind a porch support beam. *What's this?*

The orc Black Guard kept his arm around Gorva and led her down the street, talking her up with every step that she took. They finally vanished through the swinging doors of a tavern with a corner entrance a few streets down.

Grey Cloak's nimble fingers needled his palms.

This is odd. He scratched his eyebrow. *He's an orc. She's an orc. Maybe they are acquainted. Maybe they are too acquainted.*

Several potential tragic scenarios crossed his mind.

If Tanlin knows I'm here, perhaps he's trying to trap me, and

Gorva is bait. Hmm... They could slip out through a back exit. He looked down both ends of the street and checked the rooftop for yonders. *All clear. Maybe too clear.*

He pinched his cloak by the neck and lowered the hood over his eyes. Cold and damp, he missed the comfort and warmth that the Cloak of Legends had brought him. He'd shed water like a duck, and even his toes never became damp or cold. He gritted his teeth and started to venture across the sloppy street toward the tavern.

Donkey Skulls. I'm going in.

11

GREY CLOAK DIDN'T MAKE it halfway across the street before a familiar voice caught his ear.

"I wouldn't do that if I were you. She's a big orc. She can take care of herself."

He spun around. A figure stood in the shadows of the alley.

He changed direction and approached. Peering through the misty rain into the alley, he asked, "Zora?"

She stepped into full view. "Who else makes sneaking up on you look so easy? I've been tailing you for blocks."

He got boot to boot with her. "I knew you were there."

"No, you didn't." Zora wrapped her arms around him and gave him a fierce hug. "Thank the good dragons you're well! I was worried sick!"

"You don't look sick." He caressed her cheek and tickled

her earlobe. "I've missed those pretty eyes of yours. Prison changes an elf."

"Are you wooing me?"

He looked from side to side and said, "I don't see anyone else to woo aside from leaky downspouts."

"You're a little young for me." She moved his hand away from her face. "And seeing how you haven't aged in ten years, it only makes matters worse."

"You aren't going to hold that against me, are you?"

"There are more important matters at the moment." She turned him around to face the tavern. "Your friend said that she could handle herself. She's very charming."

"She's something, all right. Gorva shared the prisoner galleon with us on the trip to the island and proved to be a very worthy ally." He stood on tiptoe and craned his neck. "What is she doing in there?"

"Sergeant Slot asked her to have dinner. She didn't have a choice and played along. But I'm not so sure that she can handle the likes of him. He's no one to fool with. He's dangerous and hasn't been bashful about putting his paws on me a time or two."

"All the more reason to get her out of there," he said. "Let's go around back and make sure they don't slip out."

He crossed the street and ducked into the next alley over, avoiding a puddle of muck, and covered his nose from the stink.

"I promise when we finally have dinner, I'll take you to a place that won't smell so bad."

"How thoughtful of you," she replied as she hopped over a puddle and nearly landed on a black cat, which screeched and bounded away. "Eek! I didn't see that cat. Speaking of which, how is Streak? I take it he found you."

"He's about," Grey Cloak said. "No worries."

"I hope he's not too close. There are Riskers everywhere. Even the runt dragons the citizens own are accounted for. The farther away he is from here, the better."

The end of the alley joined a narrow street that ran along the back of the tavern. Grey Cloak stopped and shielded Zora behind him. Several men were outside the tavern's back door, smoking cigars and moving out waste bins. A Black Guard stood nearby. It wasn't Sergeant Slot, though. It was another man who was smoking a pipe.

"Do the Black Guard hang out here often?"

"They are like flies. They are everywhere." She pulled him back into the alley. "Don't let them see you. They are as nosy as old cranes too."

"Keep your ears open."

He eased back into the alley and put his back to the wall. Zora stood across from him.

"So, I hear that you killed Sash and Honzur."

Zora's eyebrows rose. "It was an awful moment. And I had some help."

"You risked it all to save Streak. I'm grateful, but wasn't Tanlin in trouble? That's why you returned, isn't it?"

She nodded. "Tanlin had it under control by the time I made it here. Once Bull lost contact with Honzur, well, as Tanlin explains it, Bull, not being so smart, was lost."

"Where is Bull now? Dead?"

"You know we aren't killers. It wasn't easy, but Tanlin used his connection with Baron Dorenzo to have Bull taken to prison. He set the entire scene up as a robbery, and Bull was hauled off like a commoner."

Grey Cloak tilted his head over his shoulder and said, "That worked out nicely. What about Squirrel and Katrina? Any word from them?"

"No. As far as I know, they are still in Harbor City. What's wrong, Grey Cloak? You don't sound like you're convinced. Do you doubt me?"

"No, no, of course not." He opened his hands in a peaceful gesture. "I'm elated. You battled the Scourge and survived. Both you and Tanlin are alive and well. I couldn't be happier, really. You know that."

She leaned her head over her shoulder and said, "I'm not convinced you believe me."

"I'm not feeling myself, Zora. Not since I lost the cloak."

"Don't make excuses." She crossed the alley and poked him in the chest. "You don't think I could take down the Scourge by myself, do you?"

"Of course I do. It was a brave thing that you did, but—"

"Don't 'but' me! I risked my life for you and your dragon. I raced back here to save Tanlin, and you doubt my intentions."

"Keep your voice down."

"Don't tell me what to do!"

A Black Guard appeared at the end of the alley. "What is the problem? This isn't a place for lovers' quarrels. Scoot your boots, both of you, or I'll haul you to the magistrate's court."

"So sorry," Grey Cloak said. He quickly turned his back to the soldier and pointed Zora the same way. "My lady has had too much to drink. I'll take her home now."

Zora threw him an elbow. "Too much to drink! I ought to—"

Grey Cloak covered her mouth and said, "Now, now, watch what you say. It could be held against you in court." He gave the Black Guard a head shake. "So sorry. Er, enjoy your evening."

Zora broke away from him at the end of the alley at the tavern's corner entrance. "You really have a way with women, don't you?"

"Can you blame me for being careful? And you shouldn't be any different. These are dangerous times that we live in."

Zora leaned against the wall, put her hands on her knees, and sighed. "I guess you're right. I don't mean to be so sensitive, but times have been hard the last ten years—well, even longer, since before I met you."

"I'm glad you came to your senses."

She shot him a dangerous look.

He offered his hands in surrender. "Only teasing. You know I can't help it."

"Funny."

He moved beside her and looked behind him up into one of the windows. The people were enjoying themselves with song, hot food, and wine. "I bet Gorva is having a good time."

"At least one of us is."

He nudged Zora with his elbow. "Come now, you know I'm fun. Right?"

She gave him a stiff elbow in return. "I'm glad you're back. So, where is the rest of Talon?"

"In the south side of the city, Cemetery Hill, waiting. I'll take you there once Gorva slips free."

"Sounds good. I can't wait to see Dyphestive." She gave him a worried look. "He's well, isn't he?"

The window above them shattered. Sergeant Slot flew over their heads and crashed into the alley.

"Better than him." He looked up and saw Gorva climbing out of the window. She wore a tomato-red-and-gold trim dress. His mouth dropped open. "Problem."

"Problem?" Gorva hopped down into the street. She

kicked Sergeant Slot in the ribs, but he was knocked out cold. "He needs to learn his manners."

"Yes, well, we don't have time to teach them now," Grey Cloak said.

The Black Guard at the end of the alley was running their way. More Black Guards hung their heads out of the window, and others spilled out of the front of the tavern.

He pointed back down the alley. "That way! Run!"

12

GORVA TOOK THE LEAD, lowered her shoulder, and plowed over the Black Guard coming their way.

"Well done," Grey Cloak said as he raced ahead.

He came to a quick halt at the end of the alley. Behind them, half a dozen angry Black Guards shouted at them to stop.

Grey Cloak looked left and right down the narrow street. "Decisions, decisions."

"This way," Zora said after a quick tug on his elbow.

They broke left and sprinted down the rain-slick street. Despite carrying a heavier build, Zora still moved with natural elven grace and agility. She turned right, jumped over waste bins like a cat, and turned left.

The Black Guards' shouts carried down the alley.

"They are calling for reinforcements," Grey Cloak said.

"I know," Zora replied. "They call for reinforcements on everything. Don't worry about that and keep up."

"No problem there," he said. He glanced over his shoulder to see that Gorva was right on his heels, but her stride was short. "Why are you running so funny?"

"Have you ever run in a dress before? This one is too tight!" Gorva shouted at Zora.

"It's the only one I had that would fit you," Zora said. She skidded to a stop and looked down one of the main streets then pointed at the other side of the road. "Let's go."

The moment they crossed the street, Black Guard spilled into the road another block down.

"There they are!" one of them shouted.

Another guard pulled out a small horn made of bone and blew it.

They didn't stand around and wait for more soldiers to arrive. Instead, they renewed their sprint and raced down the next alley.

"Do you have a hiding spot or not?" Grey Cloak asked.

"I do."

"Is it in this city?"

"Har-har," Zora replied.

Black Guard horns could be heard echoing down the alleys and streets. They were smart soldiers, using the horns to guide one another. It would only be a matter of time before the number of troops cut off all their avenues of escape.

"There!" Zora pointed ahead.

They were in the trade district, where all the stonemasons and woodworkers exercised their craft. It was a dead area at that time of night, with plenty of places to hide. She led them into a lumber mill, stirring up the sawdust as they passed.

They hid behind a stack of logs piled eight feet high. Zora sat down, chest heaving.

"This isn't an ideal hiding place. Perhaps for children," Grey Cloak said.

"Gum up. I need to catch my breath. I feel like my lungs are going to burst," Zora said.

"Do you want me to carry you?" Gorva offered. "I'm very strong."

"It's true. She is very strong," Grey Cloak agreed. "And you don't look that heavy."

Zora narrowed her eyes at him. "Watch it. I might not be as fit as I used to be, but that doesn't mean I can't handle myself."

The Black Guards' horns sounded closer.

"They are right on top of us," Gorva said. "We need to keep moving."

Grey Cloak helped Zora to her feet. "Where is the hiding place?"

Panting, Zora said, "We need to keep going north." She gasped. "There's a cathedral that houses the diseased. They won't go there."

"You're joking, right? That's your hiding spot? An infirmary of the soon-to-be dead? No, thanks. Everyone, follow me. We'll keep running until we wear them out and they give up. We can do it. How bruised will their egos be after a bad date?"

Zora took a sharp breath and regained her composure. "They won't stop. It's all a game to them. They use horses and bring dogs."

"Skreee!"

All three of them looked up through the wood mill's skylight and watched a winged shadow pass underneath the dark clouds.

"And dragons, apparently," Grey Cloak said. "It must be a slow night. It seems they don't have anything better to do. Now they can see us from the sky. Great." His gaze swept through the wood mill. "We need to find another way out of here."

"And if we don't?" Gorva asked.

Grey Cloak shook his head. "We'll be dragon food."

13

THE BLACK GUARD crept into the wood mill and spread out. They moved quietly between the stacks of wooden planks and logs of the huge structure. Their chain mail armor clinked, and their metal weapons scraped out of their sheaths.

Grey Cloak took the lead and headed away from the host of soldiers. They kept their heads low, letting the materials hide their path. The darkness gave them excellent cover, but the soldiers lit hooded lamps.

"Zora, use the Scarf of Shadows and get out of here. Go tell Tanlin what's happening, and we'll all meet up at the cemetery where Browning was buried," Grey Cloak whispered.

"I'm not leaving you," she said.

"You have to. Gorva and I will handle this."

He peeked over a pile of planks. Several soldiers were navigating their way toward them.

Squeezing Zora's hand, he said, "Go. Please go."

"I'll get help," she said. "Don't get yourself eaten. It was nice meeting you, Gorva." She lifted the scarf over her nose and vanished.

"That was a useful trick."

Grey Cloak nodded. "Tell me about it." He glanced into the rafters and saw several spots that would be safe to hide in. "Can you climb?"

Gorva nodded.

They moved like cats to the back of the mill, lengthening the distance between them and their cautious pursuers. A ladder on the back wall led up into the storage loft. They climbed the ladder and found that the loft was loaded with shop tools and pieces of scrap wood.

Twenty feet below, the soldiers prowled through the mill, some using lanterns and others navigating the shadows. They were making a thorough search of every nook in the building.

There was a six-foot gap between joists. Grey Cloak took a giant step from one rafter to the next.

"What are you doing?" Gorva whispered.

"We are going to get behind them and slip out," he whispered back. "Make sense?"

She gave a quick nod and started walking across the joists. Her feet scraped away the wood dust, making it trickle down and land on a man's shoulders. He let out a loud sneeze.

Grey Cloak and Gorva hurried across the joists, racing beneath the rafters, which supported a ceiling that was over one hundred feet long. They were halfway across when the soldiers they passed turned their lights toward the ceiling. The funnel of light started at the end, where they climbed up and began to work their way down.

Grabbing Gorva's arm, Grey Cloak said, "Faster."

He continued running across the joists, knocking more sawdust to the ground. Gorva stayed on his heels. As the beams of light swept over the rafters and closed in, they dropped, hit the ground, and rolled forward. When they came to their feet, they sped out of the wood mill, evading the soldiers.

As they exited the lumber yard, he saw horse soldiers coming down the opposite end of the street. Hiding from view, they let the horse soldiers pass, then they dashed into the alley across the street.

"I think we made it," Grey Cloak said as he walked quickly toward the far end of the alley. "It should be a piece of cake getting out of the city now."

A Risker on the back of his middling dragon entered the far end of the alley.

Grey Cloak's blood froze in his veins. "Go back, go back, go back." He turned and bumped right into Gorva. Her eyes were fixed on a second dragon and rider that blocked the alley where they'd entered.

At the same time, both dragons let out ear-splitting screeches. The sound grew louder and turned Grey Cloak's legs to noodles. His knees buckled, and he landed on them and covered his ears.

Gorva was in the same shape he was. The tight confines of the alley amplified the dragons' harrowing shrieks.

"It's days like this I wish I'd never left Havenstock," Grey Cloak muttered.

The Riskers squeezed deeper into the alley, the dragons still shrieking.

"Skreee! Skreee!"

The jarring sound froze Grey Cloak's limbs. He couldn't move or think. *What is happening?*

"We have to get out of here!" Gorva said.

"I know!" He fought his way back to his feet in time to see the chest plates of the dragons glow the color of fire. "It looks like they are going to roast us, thanks to your bad dinner date!"

"I wasn't the one that was bad!"

The shrieking stopped.

"Surrender or be incinerated!" the Risker saddled on the dragon facing Grey Cloak called.

Grey Cloak hollered back, "I believe there has been a grave misunderstanding." He was buying time. The only way of escape was up, and he couldn't fly, and he was pretty sure that Gorva couldn't either. If they tried to climb, the dragons would torch them. "You see—"

"Silence!" the Risker yelled back. "Get on your knees and place your hands on your head."

"I don't see any way out of this," Grey Cloak admitted. If he'd had the Cloak of Legends, he could handle the dragon fire, but without it, trying anything at all would only get them killed. "We can surrender and live a little longer or run and be turned into charcoal. Do you have a preference?"

Gorva dropped to her knees and said, "We'll fight another day."

"Take off your sword belt, elf, and toss it toward me," the Risker said. "And keep your hands where I can see them."

Grey Cloak loosened his belt and tossed it at the dragon's feet then placed his hands on his head.

"That will do." The Risker sniggered and said, "Let's torch them anyway."

14

THE EYES of the Risker's dragon were like burning rubies. Smoke began to flow over its teeth and out of its mouth.

Grey Cloak and Gorva both came to their feet.

"If we are going to die, we'll die standing!" Gorva said.

"Have it your way!" the Risker said. He patted his dragon on the neck.

The dragon took in a breath. A glowing dragon charm appeared at eye level between Grey Cloak and the dragon. So did the woman holding it.

"Zora!" Grey Cloak said.

The dragon's gaze locked on the stone.

"Where did you get that?" the Risker demanded. "Give it to me!"

"Grey Cloak," Zora said as her hand trembled, "I don't know what I'm doing."

He and Gorva moved closer to her.

"Keep it before the dragon's eyes. Don't let anything distract you," he said.

The second dragon approached from the opposite end of the alley. Its eyes were locked on the dragon charm as well.

Grey Cloak felt something burning a hole in his pants pocket. "Zooks, I forgot all about it." He'd been so obsessed with losing his cloak that he'd forgotten entirely about the dragon charm he'd found in the Burnt Hills. When he fished it out, it glowed like a star. He held it toward the other dragon, stopping its approach.

"Give me those stones!" the Risker demanded.

"What do we do?" Zora asked.

"I've never used one before. Tell them to stay back, but don't ask them to do something they wouldn't like or that would make them hurt themselves," he said, recalling his training at Hidemark. There, he'd learned about the dragon charms and how they could be used. Riskers that didn't bond with dragons the same way as naturals like Grey Cloak could use them. "Let me try something."

While Zora kept her dragon at bay with her charm, Grey Cloak approached the other. The middling dragon was a female. He could tell by the lighter scales on her chest plate. "Easy, girl. I bet you don't like that nasty man on your back. Why don't you throw him off?"

The dragon tilted its head and made a rattling sound in its throat.

"Don't listen to him!" The Risker hit the dragon on top of the skull with his mailed fist. "You obey me!"

From behind the dragon, a tail rose like a cobra. It slipped around the Risker's waist, jerked him out of the saddle, and slammed him into the alley wall. *Smack!* The Risker was either dead or knocked out.

Grey Cloak didn't care, but he did notice a dragon charm mounted in the man's chest plate. "Gorva, get that dragon charm!" He rushed over to Zora and put his charm beside hers. They burned brighter. "Tell the dragon to toss his rider."

"Toss your rider!" she commanded.

The dragon didn't budge, but its rider stood in his saddle, holding his stone. "You have no power over me! This is my dragon! My dragon!"

Grey Cloak offered encouraging words. "Envision what you want the dragon to do. Bond with it."

She nodded.

The dragon bucked like a mule, tossing the Risker head over heels into the air. Before the man landed, the dragon's tail whipped out and batted the Risker into the wall. It whipped the Risker several times, busting the man's bones inside his armor.

Zora gasped. "Did I do that?"

"I don't think your new friend cared for his rider."

Grey Cloak hurried over to the dead Risker and took his dragon charm from him. When he turned back, the dragon was nuzzling Zora. "I think you made a new friend."

The dragon licked her with his long black tongue. Zora cringed and said, "Now what do I do?"

Grey Cloak placed his hands on her shoulders and said, "The first thing you can do is accept my apology for ever doubting you."

"I'll think about it."

"Second..." He pulled the Scarf of Shadows over her nose. "Bring Tanlin up to speed and meet us at the cemetery, the same as before."

As she faded into invisibility, she said, "How are you going to get out of here? The Black Guard will still come for you."

"Don't worry about us. We'll take the dragons," he said, patting the dragon she'd charmed on the cheek. "If he'll have us."

"You take your own dragon!" Gorva hollered down the alley. She'd climbed into the saddle of the female dragon and gripped a dragon charm. "I'm taking this one."

Grey Cloak felt a soft kiss on his cheek and heard Zora say, "See you soon, Grey Cloak."

"Soon won't be soon enough," he replied as he grabbed his sword belt and climbed into the dragon's saddle.

The Black Guard blocked off the ends of the alley and

had begun to creep in. He and Gorva turned their dragons back to back.

Gorva grinned as she locked her fingers around the reins. "I can't wait to fly. Don't you love it?"

"I hate it," he said and wrapped his fingers in the reins.

"Really?"

"Really." He rubbed his dragon's neck and said, "Let's see what you can do. Take us out of here, and feel free to use your flame."

Like charging chickens, the dragons sprinted down the alley in opposite directions. Nearing the end, they spit geysers of flames out of their mouths.

The Black Guard scrambled for their lives, racing away from the flames, which set their boots on fire. The burning men rolled across the ground and dived into water troughs.

Grey Cloak's dragon ran down the street, beating his wings and sending terror-stricken citizens running over one another to get out of his path. The dragon lifted off the ground and soared upward into the sky. Raven Cliff diminished beneath them, and Gorva and her dragon flew alongside.

"This is wonderful!" Gorva shouted with the wind tearing through her braided hair. "I love it!"

Grey Cloak's stomach turned inside out, and he said, "Good for you!"

15

SURROUNDED by the dawn sun shining down on foggy rolling hills, tombstones, and dandelions, Grey Cloak and Dyphestive stood over their old friend Browning's grave. The tombstone had the salty old warrior's name chiseled at the top, and the saying beneath it read: Dirty Acorns, I'm Dead.

Dyphestive took a knee and started scraping away the grit that had built up over the tombstone's lettering with his fingers, then he pulled out a few weeds and tossed them aside. He sniffed and said, "Of all the ones we lost, I think I miss him the most."

"He had a way about him, didn't he?" Grey Cloak added.

"Yes, he did. Very memorable." Dyphestive grabbed the

tombstone, which was slightly askew, and straightened it. "That's better."

Cemetery Hill was covered in overgrowth. When they'd first come, it was in far better shape. The grit on most of the tombstones had been cleaned away, and flowers were planted near the graves. The flower beds had all run wild. The caretakers that oversaw the grounds appeared to have moved on, leaving the dead to be covered in overgrowth and forgotten.

"I can't believe how much this place has changed in only ten years. It looks like a jungle," Grey Cloak said. "Will the rest of the world look like this if we don't take care of it?"

"The weeds will take over if you don't pull them out by the root," Jakoby said. He was sitting against a gnarled, rotting tree. "They choke the life out of everything but feed themselves until there is nothing left to feed on."

Razor chopped at the tall grasses with his sword. "Even if you cut them, they still come back. You have to kill them." He stared at the sheer cliffs that Raven Cliff rested on. "How long are we going to wait here?"

"Until Zora comes, however long that will be," Grey Cloak said. "She'll be along. Shortly, I'm sure."

Gorva paced the grounds with a scowl on her face. She hadn't cracked a smile since they landed and set the dragons free per Grey Cloak's instructions. She kept muttering with her fists bunched at her sides.

"What is the point in having a dragon charm if you can't use it?"

Grey Cloak turned his attention to her and said, "You have to let it go, Gorva. We can't run with the dragons. Black Frost will come after them. The farther away they are from him and us, the better."

"A dragon would be useful," she stated.

"Not if the dragon is dead. And no thanks to you, we have the Black Guard searching for us."

Gorva crossed her arms and glowered at him. "What is that supposed to mean?"

"You threw Sergeant Slot through a window. All you needed to do was slip out the back."

"He tried to kiss me," she said.

Razor chuckled. "I'll make a note that you don't like being kissed near windows."

"It's not funny, fool."

He bowed and rolled his wrist. "A thousand apologies."

"The point is, Gorva, your actions could have gotten us killed. No one faults you, but we have to be smart about how we act. We can't draw attention to ourselves, or all of Black Frost's forces will be after us. We have an edge while he still doesn't know that we're alive. The longer he thinks we're dead, the better."

"Well, one thing is for certain—we are in a great place for dead people," Gorva said. Her nostrils flared, and she let out a sigh. "I miss my dragon."

Grey Cloak tossed his charm in the air and caught it. "At least we have two more charms that we can use. They should come in handy like they did today."

"How come we were able to get the dragons to respond to our charms over the Riskers?" Gorva asked as she eyed her gemstone.

"Huh, I think we surprised them. That and the fact that I don't think the dragons like their riders. I learned about dragons and the charms from the Sky Riders at Hidemark and at Dark Mountain too. A rider with natural gifts can bond with a dragon without the charms. Like me and Streak. Those riders are naturals and have unique powers." He wiggled his fingertips, and tiny blue strands of lightning danced on them. "But these other riders, they aren't all naturals. They need the charms to control the dragons, and they have to be trained. Dragons have minds of their own, the same as horses but stronger. They'd rather be wild and free, but they can be tamed or broken. I think the choice between us and their riders was easy for them. Ultimately, they wanted to be free, like you and me."

Gorva nodded. "That's what this is all about, isn't it? Freedom."

Looking off into the distance, he said, "Freedom to live and choose as we please. At least, that is what drives me." He moved to a rise among the graves and spied someone coming. He recognized Zora's stride. "It's Zora."

Jakoby and Dyphestive rose and stood with Grey Cloak.

Zora was panting when she jogged up to them, pulling a small sled behind her. She stopped and put her hands on her knees.

"Are you well?" Grey Cloak asked, eyeing the sled.

"We need to go. They are looking for us everywhere, and it's only a matter of time before they come here."

"They should be more preoccupied with finding the dragons than us. It should buy us some time." Grey Cloak could hear more dragons shrieking from the roofs of the city. He shook his head. "All of this over a bad date?"

"No," Zora said, picking her pack up again. "All of this because you flew off on two dragons and two Black Guard are dead." She took a knee by the sled and removed the blanket that covered it. It was loaded with Grey Cloak's and Dyphestive's gear, which she'd taken from Harbor Lake, including Dyphestive's two-handed iron sword. "Well, grab your gear. I'm not going to drag it anymore."

Dyphestive picked up his sword and squeezed and twisted the leather grip. "I've missed my old friend."

"Good," Zora said. "You can have it."

16

IRON HILLS

THE SOUTHERN PLAINS of Westerlund ended where the Iron Hills began. Endless leagues of tall rocky hilltops created the perfect border between Sulter Slay and the Westerlund territories. The Iron Hills' rugged terrain was notorious for countless dangers such as avalanches, pitfalls, and ambushes from goblin raiders.

Talon traveled along the base of the Iron Hills, keeping its eyes on the skies for any pursuing dragons. They'd made a clean escape from Raven Cliff and kept moving nonstop on horseback toward their next destination.

Grey Cloak and Zora shared a saddle. She leaned with her cheek against his back and her arms around his waist. She talked, but it was more of a mumble.

"I mentioned the Ruins of Thannis to Tanlin to see

what he knew. He said only a fool would venture in there without a sorceress or a priest. 'Dark magic thrives in those pits. Be wary.'"

"Lucky for us, I have some magic at my disposal." Grey Cloak massaged the air with his right hand. "We'll manage. Besides, we are only going in to take a look, in case Batram sent me on a wild goose chase."

"We need a priest or sorceress like Tatiana. Someone from the Wizard Watch, Tanlin said. Do you remember the ghost we met, Bella Von May, in the hills of Crow Valley?"

He nodded. "Yes, she almost killed you. Killed us."

"Well, Tanlin says that the Ruins of Thannis will be filled with spirits like her and even worse."

"Has Tanlin ever been there?"

"No."

"Well, he could be wrong."

"And if he isn't?"

"I'll take my chances."

Jakoby stood on the banks of the Inland Sea River, watching the water disappear into the plunging depths of the Outer Ring. He was joined by the others, who stood beside him, marveling at the great expanse between them and the edges of Monarch City.

"Home never looked so far away," he said.

A stone overlook vast enough to hold the entire group was wedged between the river and the rocks of the Iron Hills. They moved out onto it.

Razor looked over the edge and asked, "Grey Cloak, do you even have any idea where to find this place? All I see is a giant watery pit. How are we supposed to find a city that is buried? I don't see an entrance."

"No, but we know that there have been expeditions there before," Jakoby said.

Razor shook his head. "No, we've *heard* that there have been expeditions. But how do we know if we weren't on one?"

"Don't be a fool. It is well-known that men ventured into Thannis and never came back. How else can you explain so many people that are missing?"

Razor pointed down into the Outer Ring and said, "Maybe they fell down there!"

Jakoby gripped the pommel of his sword. "I tire of your petty comments."

"Go ahead and draw, big fella," Razor replied as his fingers drummed on the pommels of his swords. "I'd love to see how good you really are."

Dyphestive stepped between them. "Enough squabbling. If either one of you wants to fight, you're going to have to go through me. I suggest you settle your egos."

Razor waved him off. "All is well. Only bickering." He

patted his belly. "Besides, I'm getting hungry. I wouldn't mind a plate of hog chops and eggs. A flagon of ale wouldn't hurt too. There is a small town north of here. They make a good biscuit."

Grey Cloak moved along the rim of the stone overlook. "It's not a bad idea. Someone in the area must know something if other expeditions have passed through as you say. It wouldn't hurt to ask. Make camp, and I'll head into town with Zora and ask some questions."

"I'm coming too," Razor insisted.

"I want to go," Gorva said.

"Hold your horses. It's a small town. We can't all show up and spook them. Let Zora and me handle that."

"There won't be any need for any of that."

"Really?" Grey Cloak asked as he spun on his heel and faced the source of the objection. "And why is that —you!"

Several members of Talon gasped.

The ghostly form of Dalsay stood among them. He hadn't changed since the last time Grey Cloak saw him. His eyes were intense and probing, his beard was neatly trimmed, and he wore the same black-and-grey checkered robes with golden trim on the sleeves and hem.

Gorva drew her sword. "A spirit!" She rushed Dalsay and chopped right through him.

"He's a friend, Gorva," Grey Cloak said. "At least, I hope he is." He looked Dalsay dead on. "Are you?"

"I serve the Wizard Watch, the same as I always have," Dalsay replied in a haunting voice that carried.

Grey Cloak's skin prickled. "Then why are you here?"

"I came to warn you. Do not enter Thannis the Fallen. A certain death awaits."

17

GREY CLOAK ROLLED HIS EYES. "Stop being cryptic and vague, Dalsay. Facing death is what we do. It's how we came to be here. Are you here to help us or spook us?"

"I am helping," Dalsay answered. "By telling you not to go into Thannis."

"The only way I'm not going in there is if I know for certain that the Figurine of Heroes is not in there. Do you know where the figurine is?"

"I do. It's in the Ruins of Thannis," Dalsay replied.

"Great! How do I get there?"

"*I*, you say. Very troubling. Why do you insist on using the figurine? Is it for your gain or for the gain of others?"

Feeling his company's eyes on him, Grey Cloak pointed at his chest and said, "It's not for *me*. I need it to get rid of the underlings. They killed Tatiana. I'd think that you'd want to be rid of them too."

"Tatiana is not dead," Dalsay stated.

Zora's face lit up, and she asked, "She lives?"

"Indeed," the wizard replied.

Grey Cloak gave Dalsay a doubtful look and said, "She's not a ghost, is she?"

Dalsay shook his head. "No, she is very much alive but is enslaved by the underlings now. She's been searching for you all these years, or at least I have, for her benefit."

Tatiana and Grey Cloak had had their differences, but it warmed his heart to know that she was still alive. She'd risked her life in the towers so that he and Dyphestive could escape.

"Well, this is easy," Dyphestive said. "If we get the figurine, we can free Tatiana. We owe her that much."

"No," Dalsay said. "Tatiana sent me to find you to warn you to let this matter play out. The Figurine of Heroes is too dangerous. It took death for me to understand why, but finally, I agree with Tatiana. Leave the figurine be. The underlings, Verbard and Catten, are more preoccupied with controlling the Time Mural and leaving for their world than staying on this one."

"Are you telling me that those fiendish men are going to leave of their own accord and let us be?" Grey Cloak asked with an incredulous look. "Certainly you know better than that, Dalsay. They serve Black Frost, don't they? He won't let that happen. He needs them."

Dalsay shook his head and said, "No, he doesn't. The Wizard Watch is all but destroyed. Our craft is abandoned. The underlings saw to that in exchange for working on the Time Murals. Tatiana aides them in hopes they will soon depart. She is close."

"She is a fool, Dalsay!" Grey Cloak poked his finger through the ghost's face. "And you are a fool too. If anything, you are doing the underlings' bidding by trying to talk us out of it."

"I don't serve the underlings! I serve the Watch!" Dalsay fired back.

"No, you serve yourselves. Anya warned me about your kind, and I'd have been wise to listen. If I'd never entered that tower, the last ten years never would have happened. We wouldn't be in the mess we're in." His cheeks burned. "Tatiana took me in there, and look what happened."

Dyphestive placed his arm over Grey Cloak's shoulder and led him away. "Easy, Grey. I think Dalsay is trying to help in his own... well, mysterious way."

"Every time they stick their noses in our affairs, the worst happens."

"That's not true. You know they've been there for us."

"Really, Dyphestive? You think so? I don't." He slipped away from Dyphestive and placed his attention square on Dalsay. "Will you show us the way to the ruins or not?"

"I will, but I must warn you—"

"I know. Death will come. Show us the way."

Dalsay nodded. "You'll have to leave the horses. And most of your gear. The trek is dangerous." He walked across the overlook and into the air as if he were on an invisible bridge then turned to face them and pointed down at the rock. "There is the path."

Grey Cloak leaned over the overlook and craned his neck. A narrow ledge with handholds could be seen on the face of the drop-off. It zigzagged back and forth over one hundred feet and vanished underneath the waterfall created by the Inland Sea River. He shook his head, leaned back up, and said, "I hope everybody likes to climb."

The entire group took a long look over the edge.

"Ah, I see it," Gorva said. She'd suited back up in her leather armor, which Zora had returned to her. "I've climbed worse."

Razor whistled and said, "I haven't. Looks like we're going to need a really long rope." He caught everyone looking at him. "What? I'm a swordsman, not a mountain goat. What about you, Jakoby? Do you think you can climb down that like a squirrel?"

Jakoby shook his head. "No, I'll be using a rope."

Dyphestive had already started tying a rope to his horse's saddle. He threw the rope over the rim and gestured to Jakoby and Razor. "After you."

"Great," Razor said as he lifted the rope from the lip. "I'll go first."

"What about the horses? Who is going to stay with them and our gear?" Zora asked.

Razor stopped his descent and said, "Well, they are going to need protection. And seeing how I'm the best protector, I'll volunteer to stay."

"Zora, I was hoping you would stay," Grey Cloak suggested.

"If you are going to steal something, you're going to need a thief." Zora lowered herself over the rock and started to climb down. She winked at him. "See you at the bottom."

Leena slipped in right behind her, followed by Gorva. They traversed down the sheer climb, using the small handholds and narrow ledges like they'd done it one hundred times before.

Razor elbowed Grey Cloak and grinned. "You know what they say—ladies first. And it looks like I'm staying on the deck."

18

WIZARD WATCH

TATIANA LUGGED a golden jug filled with wine down the corridor. Her shoulders sagged, and her tattered wizard robes hid chains that linked her bony ankles and dragged across the floor. Her hair was a mess, and dark circles were under her eyes. She yawned and moved on, dreading her next stop in Verbard and Catten's chambers.

The towers of the Wizard Watch had been her home most of her life, and they had turned into a place of death and disaster. They had changed from being a sanctuary of beauty and splendor to a crypt with no hope for escape.

She passed a beautiful fountain whose waters had long gone dry. All the fish that had thrived in the pool were long dead. The air was stale and reeked of rotten flesh.

Life had been awful since the underlings arrived. In a matter of minutes, the devious pair took over everything.

They killed Uruiah, the highest-ranking wizard of the Watch, and destroyed her evil brood. Uruiah and her wicked brood had joined forces with Black Frost and betrayed the Wizard Watch by coming for Grey Cloak, Dyphestive, and the Figurine of Heroes. They came to kill them all.

Tatiana never saw it coming. Her faith in the Wizard Watch was shattered.

But that wasn't the worst of her troubles. Against her objections, Grey Cloak had used the figurine to bail them out. Instead, two horrors from another world arrived and turned the tables on Uruiah. With power the likes of which Tatiana had never seen, the underlings toyed with the Wizard Watch and blasted them out of existence. But the victory for good was short-lived. As the underlings started to fade, they sent the Figurine of Heroes through the Time Mural, allowing their essence to stay. Grey Cloak, Dyphestive, and Streak fled into the mural and were lost, and Tatiana was trapped.

The underlings spared her and her mentor, Gossamer. But the life she'd known would never be the same.

"Hurry along, elf woman," Catten called as she passed through an archway and entered their chamber. It was same chamber where the Time Mural was hidden from view with curtains. "I swear, you become slower by the day. Pick it up. I thought elves were supposed to be quick."

Tatiana hurried into the room.

Verbard and Catten sat side by side on two pewter thrones fashioned for them. They were small in build and had grey skin and fine rat-like fur. The hair on their heads was coarse and black, their teeth were sharp, and the pointed tips of their fingernails needled the armrests of their chairs. Both of them wore pitch-black robes with traces of silver patterns in the lining. The only features that set them apart were their eyes. Catten's irises were pure gold, and Verbard's were as polished as silver, but the latter's head was rounder.

Verbard sat to the left of Catten, and he twirled a black cane with a silver ball tip that had once belonged to the former high wizard of the tower, Gossamer.

The chains binding Tatiana's feet moved with a life of their own and tripped her. She stumbled and fell, hitting her knee hard on the ground as the carafe of wine bounced off the floor and spilled all over.

"You clumsy fool!" Verbard said. "We demand wine, and you spill it all over. What is wrong with you, elf woman? Why can't you keep your feet?" He tapped the cane on the floor. "Answer me!"

"I'm sorry." Tatiana pushed up on her trembling bony arms. "I-I tripped. I'll clean it up right away." She set the golden carafe upright and started wiping up the spilled wine with her robes. She kept her eyes down and said, "I'll fetch more."

Verbard leaned forward and said, "Listen to her, brother. She speaks to us as if she is an equal."

"No, master, I—"

Whack! Verbard hit her across the back with his cane. "I am not your master. I am Lord Verbard. He is Lord Catten. How ignorant are you?"

Tatiana sobbed. "I'm sorry. I am weary. I forget... Lord."

Whack!

"Aaauuggh!" she cried and collapsed onto the floor.

"Why do you torment her so much?" Catten asked. "If you break her back, she won't be able to serve our purposes."

"I like to hear her scream. It's delightful. And her shrieks have a special ring to them. They're music to my ears." Verbard leaned back and made himself comfy in his pillowed chair. "Up, elf woman. Fetch us more port from the wine cellar. I'm tired of your watery wine. I need something stronger."

Tatiana rose, kept her eyes down, and said, "As you wish, Lord Verbard. I'll hurry."

She had more marks on her back than she could count, but she didn't care. The more vulnerable she seemed, the greater trust she could gain. Ever since the underlings had taken over, she played the part of a feeble sorceress, all but helpless without the Star of Light, which Lord Catten wore around his neck. Her plan had allowed her to live thus far.

Others that showed defiance or joined the underlings were tormented and oftentimes killed quickly.

Gossamer entered the room. The last ten years had worn the formerly young-looking elf's face. Crow's-feet were in the corners of his eyes, and he had burn marks on his cheeks from the power in Catten's clawed fingers. His long hair, which had once been neatly parted with strands of white on one side and black on the other, had grown out and mixed together. His black-and-white checkered robes were worn and frayed at the hem. Chains rattled underneath his robes when he walked farther inside, politely bowed, and made an announcement. "Lord Catten and Lord Verbard, we have visitors that seek your audience on the roof."

Catten asked, "Who is on our roof?"

"It is the leaders of the Riskers, Commander Dirklen and his sister, Commander Magnolia. They seek your audience."

"Who?" Verbard asked his brother.

"Humans, the ones who ride the dragons," Catten replied.

"Oh," Verbard said as he waved Gossamer on. "They'll have to wait."

19

THE WINE CELLAR in the bowels of the tower filled an entire floor. Racks of wooden shelving started on the outer ring of the circular room and surrounded a smaller ring, creating wine rack after wine rack toward the center, where only one small ring of wine bottles remained.

Tatiana navigated through the maze of wine racks, which towered above her. The shelves were filled with wines from cities in every one of the nine territories, collected over the centuries. Some bottles were over a thousand years old and had labels written in a language that was long forgotten.

She removed two ancient bottles of port and wiped the dust away from the green glass with a towel. The sound of rattling chains caught her ear, and she turned. "Gossamer, you shouldn't be down here."

"I wanted to see how you're doing. I saw what Verbard did to you."

"My skin's thick. I can take it." She navigated back toward the exit, where a drinking lounge was located, then grabbed an empty crystal carafe from one of the bars and emptied the bottle of port into it. "They like crystal. They won't break it. Do you know why the Troubled Twins have arrived?"

"No," he said, sweeping his long hair over his pointed ears, "but I find it humorous that the underlings are keeping them waiting. They have little regard for anyone in this world at all. Anyone else would be rolling out the red carpet to let them in."

"That's why I want to be up there when they are given an audience. I want to see what they have to say." She brushed by Gossamer and briefly embraced him. "Stay strong."

He nodded.

Tatiana went back to the Time Mural chamber and filled the underlings' goblets to their rims.

Verbard sipped his goblet halfway down before Catten even touched his. "You'd better drink, brother. You know how wordy these humans can be." His eyes slid over to Tatiana, who stood nearby with her arms behind her back. Gossamer was in the room with her. "I see you brought a second bottle, but it won't be a gift for our guests. No, their gift is an audience with me."

"Yes, Lord Verbard," she said.

"Hmm," he grunted. "Life is so much better than death, except for times like this. Shall we see them in and get this over with?"

Catten fiddled with the Star of Light. The diamond twinkled in his fingers. "Agreed. Bring them in. And see to it that they are properly examined. There is always a chance they are imposters stowing away the figurine."

"As you wish, Lord Verbard." Gossamer hurried away and vanished through the archway.

Verbard's fingernails needled his metal armrest, making tiny divots in the metal and creating a sound like rain on a roof. "The sooner we depart this world, the better. Imagine, a world without underlings. How miserable."

Catten took his first sip of port and said, "Patience, brother. It's only a small matter of time until we master the Time Mural, then we'll be reunited with our family."

Verbard bared his teeth and replied, "And vengeance will be ours."

A few minutes later, Gossamer announced the arrival of Dirklen and Magnolia, who stormed into the room and stood before the underlings. They were a handsome pair with wavy blond hair down past the shoulders. Tatiana had seen the pair on and off over the years. They towered over the underlings.

"How dare you search us, underlings?" Dirklen poked his finger at both of them. "We are not commoners! We are the rulers of this world, your allies, and you treat us like the enemy! Apologize!"

Verbard cocked his head, tapped his fingertips together, and said, "I don't know the meaning of the word."

Dirklen pulled his sword free.

Verbard's fingertips danced with lightning. "One more step, human, and I will cook you inside and out."

Dirklen's long sword flared with mystic fire. "Don't trifle with me, underling. One poke from my steel, and I'll end you. And I'll feed you to my dragon too."

"Enough of this puffery," Magnolia said as she pushed Dirklen's sword down. "We'll make Black Frost fully aware of this insubordination. If they don't want to cooperate, I'm certain he'd be glad to tear the top off this candle they hide in and let them fend for themselves."

The fire on Verbard's fingertips died, and he cowered behind his hands. "Oh no, please don't abandon me in the world full of inferior people that I can destroy with a thought." His smug look returned. "Are you finished letting your feelings be hurt, human?"

"It's Dirklen!"

"Dirklen, human... all of you look the same to me." Verbard swallowed the rest of his port. "Ah, now, will you put away your sword and share your business? You are interrupting very important work."

Magnolia and Dirklen glanced over their shoulders as

the curtains drew in from the Time Mural and shook their heads.

"Yes, you appear to be very busy in this very empty room," Magnolia said.

Dirklen sheathed his sword, but the prickly atmosphere remained. "We have news. A common enemy has resurfaced after all these years."

"Common enemy? Interesting. I didn't think we had any," Verbard replied. "And who might they be?"

Tatiana's back straightened. Out of the corner of her eye, she noticed Gossamer slightly turn his ear. Her heart leapt when she heard Magnolia say, "Grey Cloak and Dyphestive have returned."

20

VERBARD OFFERED Catten a puzzled look and asked, "Who is this human talking about, and why should we be concerned?"

"Do you remember when we arrived?" Catten turned his gaze on Magnolia. "I believe the human is referring to the elf that summoned us. He is the one called Grey Cloak, is he not?"

"Precisely," she said.

Verbard's back straightened. "Does he have the figurine?"

"Ah, *now* you're interested in what we have to say. My, how the tables have turned, underling," Dirklen said while offering a cocky smirk that drew a deep frown from Verbard and Catten.

Tatiana tingled all over. She'd hoped that Grey Cloak

and Dyphestive had survived and would reappear again. The fact that they had was nothing short of a miracle. She'd been able to communicate with Dalsay in secret, and he'd been searching for years for the brothers. At least she could tell him they were out there, if he had not found them already.

Finally, we have a chance against these fiends.

She'd given Dalsay orders to tell the brothers to stay away from the Wizard Watch. The underlings would see them coming from leagues away. As long as the underlings remained inside the towers, the evil brothers were protected from the figurine's powers. It was imperative that the figurine didn't make it within the tower's arcane walls.

But that wasn't the only reason Tatiana wanted the brothers to stay away. The underlings were brilliant magicians with great minds and were testing the Time Mural's powers and learning how to control it. If they mastered the Time Mural and returned to their home, it was possible that she could use the Time Mural to defeat Black Frost once and for all. She needed that knowledge, and she would do anything to get it.

The underlings rose from their chairs and floated, glowering down at the twins. The hems of their robes hung inches above the floor, but their feet could not be seen. They moved toward the twins.

Dirklen and Magnolia stepped back.

Verbard stuck his nose down in Dirklen's face. "Where are these nuisances?"

"Oh, now you want our help, I see," Dirklen said as he returned a smile. "The truth of the matter is that I don't know exactly where they are. I only know where they have been."

"Don't toy with me, human," Verbard warned. "I'll fry your grey matter with a thought."

Dirklen's jaw muscles clenched, his nostrils flared, and he leaned into Verbard's face. "Listen to me, Port Breath. We have an alliance. Your purpose and our purpose is one, and you are only here because Black Frost allows it. He has a vested interest in you and this portal. Do your duty, and we will take care of ours."

"We can't do our duty if the elf shows up with the figurine, human," Verbard said. His right index finger glowed red-hot like metal in a forge, and he held it by Dirklen's face.

Sweat beaded above on the Risker's brow.

"Put an end to these people."

"Rest assured that our finest hunters are tracking them down as we speak. It's only a matter of time before we catch up with them, if we haven't already." Dirklen brushed the underling's hand away from his face. "And if you ever stick that finger in my face again, I'll cut it off and feed it to you. Come on, Magnolia. We have better things to do."

As quickly as they arrived, Dirklen and Magnolia departed, with Gossamer trailing after them.

Tatiana hadn't smiled in years, but she smiled on the inside as a warm feeling washed through her. *They're rattled. Who better to do it than Grey Cloak and Dyphestive? Like halfling beggars, they keep showing up.*

Verbard wrung his hands. "Brother, we need to accelerate our efforts."

"I couldn't agree more." Catten waved his open hands in a smooth circular motion, and the curtains parted, revealing the archway of the Time Mural.

The ominous archway had a continuous series of images that changed in the wink of the eye. It showed green fields, stark mountains, lagoons, and battles raging on other worlds.

Tatiana rubbed the goose bumps on her arms. Every time she viewed the Time Mural, a thrill went through her. More than once, she'd toyed with the idea of jumping into the mural and making a hasty escape, the same as Grey Cloak and Dyphestive had done. She had a duty, though, to the Wizard Watch and, more importantly, to her friends. Diving into the portal would be the easy way out.

Catten floated across the room to a pedestal the underlings had erected. He removed a silk blanket that covered the pedestal, revealing a square top filled with large gemstones in a variety of colors spread out evenly like they were part of a game board.

The underlings had worked tirelessly on the Time Mural pedestal and its pieces. They'd invested a great deal of time enchanting each and every gemstone they recovered from the Wizard Watch's vaults. The vast majority of the gemstones were carefully embedded in the archway stones of the Time Mural. Diamonds, rubies, emeralds, amethysts, jade, moonstones, and garnets the size of eyeballs accompanied finger-wide bricks of gold, silver, and copper that filled the gaps between the arch's stones.

Catten plucked a diamond the size of his finger from the pedestal then rolled it between his palms and said, "Are you ready to try again, brother?"

Verbard's slender fingers massaged his chin. "I've been meditating long enough. It's time to conquer our destiny." His eyes slid over to Tatiana. "Elf woman, come here. Your day has come."

21

RUINS OF THANNIS

BEHIND THE WATERFALL created by the Inland Sea river, a cave-like passage was burrowed into the rock. Led by the luminous form of Dalsay, the members of Talon began a slow descent into darkness over one hundred feet below the ground.

They'd been walking for hours through the narrow passage, which was barely three shoulder breadths wide. At the front, Dyphestive and Jakoby walked with their necks bent and their shoulders hunched.

"You wouldn't happen to know how much farther it is, would you, Dalsay?" Grey Cloak asked. "It's not as if my feet are sore or anything, but the scenery is very bleak."

"The edges of Thannis stood leagues away from the edge of the Outer Ring before the Iron Hills swallowed it,"

Dalsay replied without looking back. "At this pace, it will be hours longer."

"Huh, I don't suppose there are any tavern stops along the way," Dyphestive quipped.

Without a word, Dalsay continued his brisk pace. Even without a solid body, he still walked through the passage as men did.

Grey Cloak caught Dyphestive looking back at him and gave him a shrug, which Dyphestive returned. He knew what Dyphestive was thinking. Dalsay was a cryptic sort, and he kept the true intent of his missions tight to his chest. Grey Cloak hadn't liked that when they first met him, and he still didn't. Members of the Wizard Watch, like Dalsay and Tatiana, had played games then and were still playing them.

"Tell me, Dalsay, how is it that you know that the Figurine of Heroes is hidden in these depths?" Dyphestive asked.

"Good question," Grey Cloak agreed.

"My answer isn't going to change the situation," Dalsay said.

"I don't like him," Gorva, who carried a torch, said quietly to Zora. "He's misleading."

"Most wizards are," Zora replied.

"Now isn't the time to build mistrust, Dalsay!" Grey Cloak said. "We've all been through enough. Tell me, tell *us*, how you know for certain that the figurine rests down here... somewhere."

"What makes you think that it is down here?" Dalsay replied.

"If you aren't going to help, why are you here?"

"I didn't come to help. I came to warn you." Dalsay stopped and turned. "If you insist—"

"I do," Grey Cloak replied and caught approving looks from his comrades. "We all do."

Dalsay nodded and said, "I know the figure is here because you told me."

"That's impossible. You're repeating the lie that Batram gave me," he said. "It couldn't have been me, because I've been with Dyphestive ever since it was lost. We're going to need a better explanation than that, Dalsay."

"I don't have a greater explanation to give you. It was you that told me it was here." Dalsay turned and resumed his trek.

Grey Cloak caught everyone looking at him. He threw up his hands and said, "It wasn't me. I swear it. I think. Dyphestive and I haven't been apart since we jumped through the Time Mural. Right, Dyphestive?"

"You haven't been out of my sight." Dyphestive wiggled his eyebrows. "Maybe the Time Mural made another one of you." A whimsical smile crossed his face. "Maybe it made another one of me."

"Two Grey Cloaks?" Zora rolled her eyes. "As if one didn't get us in enough trouble."

"Goy," he said as Zora pushed by him and smirked. "You'd be lucky if there were two of me. You all would."

The company moved as one, leaving Grey Cloak talking to himself in the dark.

"Two of me... huh, now that would be interesting."

Over a league of nonstop walking came to an end where the passage bottomed out in an endless black cavern with a huge field covered in glowing dandelions with floating white seeds.

Zora bent over and plucked one. "It's beautiful." She blew the white floaties away, and they drifted in the air. "How can they live in darkness?"

"Where there is death comes life," Dalsay said. "Such is the way with seeds. There is life in the soil here. Follow. We must be close."

The wizard passed right through the dandelions without disturbing a single one. Dyphestive and Jakoby walked right behind him, kicking up bright seeds by the thousands and clearing a path for the others.

Dyphestive had a huge grin on his face as he blew the seeds away from his face and gave a hearty chuckle. "I wonder why they aren't like this on the top side of the world."

"Who knows," Zora said while catching the floating seedlings. "But I wish they were."

The seeds' light lasted for several seconds before it died out and the seeds landed on the ground again.

"Ah," Dyphestive said.

Grey Cloak followed the group from the rear, taking note of the black path they left behind between the shimmering fields of strange dandelions.

Zora drifted back beside him and asked, "Isn't it the most wonderful thing you ever saw?"

"It's taking all I have to contain my excitement," he admitted.

"I'm sure it is." She reached down and held his hand. "My tummy is telling me that we need to make the most of it. I imagine this delightful walk through the fields won't last that long." She caught him glancing over his shoulder. "Why do you keep looking back?"

"I'm wondering if we've reached the point of no return."

"Don't say that." She squeezed his hand. "I have faith in you. You'll think of something."

Grey Cloak tightened his grip. "I know."

As he walked, Dyphestive spun around, looking upward, and said, "It looks like the night sky without stars. There is no top to it. Why hasn't the world above fallen in on the world below?"

"Gapoli is rich in leagues of great tunnels and caverns in the earth, more than the races could explore in a hundred lifetimes," Dalsay said. "Fortunately for us, we are only looking for one spot in the bowels of the earth." He pointed his ghostly finger outward as everyone stood in a row beside him. "And there it is. There, my friends, is Thannis."

In the open field among the dandelions were huge piles of rubble, rocks, and ruins. Most of them were covered in green moss that glowed like the dandelions and outlined the surviving structures of the fallen city.

"It's so quiet," Zora said as she rubbed her nose. "Almost peaceful, but I have chill bumps all over me." She swallowed. "Are we going in there?"

The grim-faced Dalsay slowly nodded. "But from here on out, exercise silence."

"I thought you said this place was filled with the undead," Grey Cloak said. "But we haven't seen anything but flowers."

"The dead slumber, but remember this. Wake up one, and we wake them all and become one with their armies," Dalsay warned.

22

ZORA WASN'T the only one with chills as they waded into the ruins of the fallen city. They broke out all over Grey Cloak.

Get it together, elf. Get it together. You don't need the cloak.

The Cloak of Legends had become a crutch for him over the years, and he felt naked without it. It gave him protection and a feeling of invincibility like he'd never felt before. Now he only had his skin and bones to protect him.

To make matters worse, he had to rely on his friends more to see the mission through. That meant putting their lives at risk, which was the last thing he wanted to do. *If I had my way, I'd do it all by myself.*

With Zora shadowing him, he crept along strange ridges and structures that had been long buried by time. The faint outline of old streets made a rough-hewn pattern through the city in some spots. Strange vegetation aside, there wasn't any sign of anyone, living or dead, aside from them.

It's hard to believe someone couldn't find their way out of this. There's nothing here.

Everyone walked the grounds, looking for an entrance to something, and that was the problem. They'd been searching through the piles of rubble and fallen pillars without finding anything. Even Dalsay had a perplexed expression on his long face.

Nearby, Dyphestive and Jakoby sat on a pile of rocks, sharing a canteen of water. Leena hovered behind Dyphestive's broad back.

Grey Cloak scratched behind his ear and shrugged at Zora.

She mouthed, "There isn't anything down here. Dalsay is crazy."

She might not have been too far off the mark. Perhaps Dalsay wanted them out of the way, and he'd led them to a trap. After all, many of the Wizard Watch had turned and served Black Frost. Grey Cloak approached Dalsay, only to see him vanish inside a fallen structure half-buried under stone.

He did that on purpose. I know he saw me coming.

They'd been combing the area for hours without finding any evidence that would lead them to the Figurine of Heroes. Grey Cloak held his chin and tapped his cheek with his index finger. *If I had been here before, where would I hide the figurine? Wouldn't that be something if I was here before? Could there really be two of me? And if there were two, could there be three or possibly four or more? Oh my, I'm getting giddy.*

Grey Cloak traipsed toward a pile of rocks that had crushed what looked like a wooden barn. He'd been past it a dozen times before.

I've hidden plenty of things, and often, the best place is in plain sight. That's what I'd do.

He peered at the pile of rubble and noticed that several of the planks were still intact and lying side by side in a neat row. There were several stones the size of a man's head resting on top of them. Moss covered them, and dandelions grew among them. The odd thing about the stones was that they were shaped almost like horseshoes, and he hated shoeing horses.

"What are you staring at?" Zora whispered in his ear.

He pointed at the formation of stones and made a U-shaped pattern in the air. "For some reason, that seems oddly familiar. What do you think?"

"I think those stones look too heavy for you to lift," she said.

"Funny." He stepped onto the mossy planks and felt them slightly bow. He picked up a stone and said, "Help me out," to Zora.

She took the stone from him and gently set it on the

ground. He continued to pull the stones away from their mossy nests and hand them to Zora, who groaned as she cradled each and every one and set them down.

"Next time, use your brother for manual labor." She placed her hands on the back of her hips and arched backward. "These things are killing my back." She caught him looking at her chest, furrowed her brow, and asked, "What are you looking at?"

"Me? Nothing." He smirked as he knelt on the planks. "Only it's a shame your back hurts. Next time, I'll remember to use smaller stones."

She playfully smacked him in the back of the head and said, "Get to work."

He scraped away the moss with his fingers until he found the outlines between the individual boards. Then he wiggled one in the middle free and peeled it away from its home in the dirt.

"Did you find something?" Dyphestive asked.

"Shh," Zora said.

Dyphestive lowered his voice to a whisper and asked, "Sorry, did you find something?"

"Perhaps," Grey Cloak said. He grunted as he struggled to pull the next plank of wood up. It was wedged firmly in the ground.

"Here, let me help." Dyphestive bent over, grabbed the board with one hand, and started to lift it from its grave.

"Easy!" Grey Cloak warned.

The wooden plank made a loud sound as it rubbed against the others and came free. The ground slipped at the top of the plank, and a small boulder rolled into the pitch-black gap. Stone smacked against stone as it plunged into the darkness. *Clack. Clack. Clack.*

Grey Cloak looked up at his brother and said, "Well done, Dyphestive. Well done. Now the dead will know that we're here."

Dyphestive leaned over the gap. "What makes you think the dead are down there? It's only a hole in the ground. It's probably noth—urk!"

A mossy tendril spotted with thorns came out of the darkness, coiled around Dyphestive's neck, and yanked him into the pit.

"Dyphestive!" Grey Cloak shouted into the gap. His voice echoed back. "Dyphestive, I'm coming!"

23

Grey Cloak started to jump into the gap, but Jakoby hooked his arm and hauled him back. "Don't be a fool. You don't know what lies down there. Exercise some discipline, or we'll all be dead."

"Let go of me. The longer we wait, the farther it gets away," he said, yanking his arm out of Jakoby's grasp.

Dalsay stood over the pit, hovering in the air, and said, "Jakoby is right. We must exercise caution. I'll go forward and see what has befallen him. It cannot hurt me."

But Leena jumped right through Dalsay and vanished into the dark hole.

"Oh no, she's not going to rescue my brother before me." Grey Cloak jumped in after her and landed on a rock several feet below. It created a crude staircase that led into the depths of the fallen city.

He hurried after her and caught up dozens of feet below. "Wait, Leena."

Dalsay dropped between them. His ghostly form created a dull illumination that revealed a passage made of broken walls and dirt. There were drag marks on the ground that followed the passage.

Grey Cloak drew his sword and dagger and said, "I'm not standing around and waiting for the others to get down here."

He and Leena made their way down the passage.

Dalsay soared by them, turned, and asked, "Will you let me lead this expedition? As I said, they cannot harm me. Wait here and give me a moment to find him."

"If you find him, you can't help him," Grey Cloak said. "Whatever took him is strong and fast. You'll need our help to fight it."

Dalsay glared at him. "Whatever sort of creature took him won't be alone either. I warned you about the need for silence. Listen to the clamor."

Grey Cloak could hear the others making their way down the rocks. There was panting, heavy breathing, footsteps scuffling on rock, and the rattle of Jakoby's armor. He stormed back down the passage and whispered through his teeth, "Stay put. Dalsay, Leena, and I will go forward."

"You don't have a torch. I have a torch. I should lead you," Gorva said.

"Dalsay is our torch, and I have other methods. We'll return shortly," he said.

Zora gave him a worried look and said, "You have an hour. Hurry."

He caught up to Leena and Dalsay, who had moved farther down the passage.

We're coming, brother. We're coming.

The tendril pulled Dyphestive into the inky depths and kept going. He bounced off stone landing after stone landing and hit the ground, still being dragged by the neck.

Whatever had ahold of him moved fast and had great strength. The strands coiled around Dyphestive's neck and squeezed hard. The thorns dug into his flesh, sinking deeper and deeper. They would have broken the neck of a lesser man and snapped it like a twig.

Dyphestive was a natural and no ordinary man. He flexed his bull neck and sank his head deeper into his shoulders. One hand remained locked on the handle of his sword. The other hand was free.

Whatever you are, you won't have me today. This isn't the first time I've been dragged.

The Doom Riders had put a rope around his neck once and dragged him behind a dragon horse called a gourn. He was reminded of that day, and the thought of it turned his blood to fire.

Using his free hand, he grabbed the thorny tentacles and squeezed. The sharp thorns pierced the skin and muscles of his palm. He kicked, trying to catch a fixed object that would slow him. The toes of his boots skipped over rough rocks that tore up his trousers and busted his knees.

He tugged on the tentacles, which were dragging him as fast as a galloping horse, and twisted over onto his belly. Though he couldn't see a thing ahead of him, he could feel the ground scraping the skin from his chest. He envisioned his hand locked around the tentacle. *Don't cut your hand off, Dyphestive.*

He lifted the iron sword from the ground, aimed for the tentacle above his hand, and brought it down hard. *Chop!*

Steel cut cleanly through the tendril, and he rolled to a stop.

Farther down the corridor, the creature let out an ear-splitting screech.

A sound like thousands of tiny feet stomping over the ground echoed down the passage and stormed toward him.

Dyphestive groaned and came up to one knee. Lost in the dark, he faced the unseen enemy charging toward him. It sounded like thousands of buzzing bees. With the painful tentacle still attached, he grabbed his sword with both hands and closed his eyes. His vision was useless in the dark. He would have to rely on his other senses, the way he'd been taught by the Doom Riders when he leaned to fight in the dark.

The creature stormed closer.

Dyphestive timed his attack, cocked his elbow, and lunged.

24

A TERRIFYING SHRIEK echoed through the expanding labyrinth of misshapen passages and caught Grey Cloak's ear. He raced straight through Dalsay's body, with Leena on his heels, only to see Dalsay sail back through both of them.

"Follow me, I implore you," Dalsay said as the tips of his toes dusted over the ground and sped through the tunnel. The passage bent left and right, sloping up and down. The stone structures that held the ceiling in place looked as if they might cave in at any moment. Dalsay jabbed his fingers out from under his robes. "There."

Dyphestive knelt in the middle of the passage, grimacing. He'd begun to peel away the thorny tendril buried in his hand.

Grey Cloak rushed to his aid. "Brother, are you wounded?" He caught his first glimpse of the monster that had reeled Dyphestive into the depths and stopped in his tracks. He brandished his blades.

"It's dead," Dyphestive said in a hoarse voice. "But this is the first look I got of it. Yuck. A nasty beast."

Blocking further passage was one of the ugliest creatures Grey Cloak had ever seen. It had thousands of legs underneath a massive wormlike body with black hair that was sharp and spiny. Oversized green eyes loomed over a gaping, oozing mouth filled with hundreds of sharp and jagged teeth. The iron sword was sunk hilt deep between its eyes. Pus from the wound leaked down its face. On its back were spiny ridges and long thorny, slimy tentacles thicker than rope.

Dyphestive pulled the tentacle out of his bloody hand and chucked it aside.

Grey Cloak grimaced. "Doesn't that hurt?"

"Yeah, but only on the inside and everywhere else." With the help of Leena, Dyphestive uncoiled the gooey strand choking his neck. It peeled away and took some skin with it.

"Ouch," Grey Cloak muttered. He watched Leena pluck black thorns from Dyphestive's thick neck. "Glad it was you and not me."

Dyphestive picked a few more thorns from the palm of his hand and said, "You might not have made it. I plowed over more rocks than I'll ever remember." He rubbed his shoulder and cracked his neck. "And I felt every one of them."

Leena dangled the severed tentacle in front of her sour face and flung it away.

Dyphestive planted his foot in the monster's face and pulled the iron sword free. "Dalsay, do you know what that thing is?"

"A cavern creeper. Very deadly. It's a wonder that you are alive," Dalsay commented. He passed through the creeper and disappeared to the other side.

Dyphestive looked like he'd been dragged behind a wagon for a league. He had cuts and scrapes all over him. His trousers were shredded. He checked his woolen vest, which was in better shape than the rest of him, and said, "Will you look at this? After all of that, the stitching still held. Remarkable, isn't it? I couldn't have stitched it better myself."

"Are you sure you're well?" Grey Cloak asked.

"Would it make any difference if I wasn't? We're still here, aren't we?"

Gorva approached quickly with a torch in one hand and a sword in the other. Wide-eyed, Zora and Jakoby were right behind her.

"What happened? We heard a shriek," Gorva said.

Dyphestive pointed at the cavern creeper. "That happened. Don't worry. It's dead now."

Zora let out a sigh. "Thank goodness. But are you well?"

"Why does everyone keep asking me that?" Dyphestive asked.

"Because you look like that monster chewed you up and spit you out." Jakoby poked the monster with his sword. "A cavern creeper. I've heard about them but didn't believe they were real. Hopefully, you killed the last of them." He hacked into its body several times with his sword and said, "You can never be too sure." He slung the gore off his blade. "Yuck. It smells worse than it looks."

For the rest of the trek, Grey Cloak let Dalsay lead the way through the passages. The last surprise had almost gotten his best friend killed, and he couldn't let that happen again.

The next time one of those cavern creepers appears, let it wrap its tentacles around Dalsay. I don't think I'd mind seeing that. I'm starting to believe wizards are nothing but trouble. I miss Anya.

Chink. Thud. Chink. Thud. Chink. Thud. Chink. Chink. Chink. Thud.

The company exchanged startled looks.

Dyphestive said, "That sounds like digging."

Dalsay picked up the pace and moved straight toward the source of the sound. The passage emptied out on a rise that overlooked an entire ancient city resting underneath a dome of stone. He clawed at his beard and said, "Welcome to Thannis."

"Dragon's breath, it's almost as big as Raven Cliff," Zora uttered. "How can this be?"

Grey Cloak shrugged.

Thannis sat under a ceiling of rock filled with quartz that glowed like starlight. It cast light on a deteriorating city of weathered buildings that had withstood the test of time. The strange light shimmered on the glassy surface of a lake between them and the city. A backdrop of rocky climbs and tunnel entrances stood behind the city. Small bodies moved along the ledges, pushing carts and carrying hammers and picks.

"Are those gnomes?" Dyphestive asked.

Many people wandered along the outskirts of the city and the streets within. But the hammering and shoveling were definitely coming from the hills.

"There's only one way to find out. *I'll* take a closer look." Grey Cloak took off before anyone had time to object. He raced down the slope as quietly as a deer and made his way around the edge of the lake. Paths had been worn in an odd mossy grass, and he followed them toward the city.

A pair of people walked toward him at a slow gait. He crouched behind a pile of rubble along the road and hid. It was a man and a woman wearing moth-eaten clothing. Their skin had deep creases beneath the cheekbones, and their eyes were almost hollowed out. Flesh had fallen from their bones. They moved slowly on their rickety limbs, holding hands with fingers that were missing.

Grey Cloak's heart started to race. He slunk farther away from the pair and scanned the grounds. The undead were everywhere—in the fields, on the streets, living out their routine lives, fishing, hammering, walking, and eating.

His skin crawled. He turned to head back up the hill to his friends and found himself face-to-face with zombies.

25

WIZARD WATCH

"Go ahead, elf woman, pick one up," the golden-eyed Catten offered. He stood on the far side of the pedestal of precious stones. "Choose whatever stone that will connect you."

Tatiana, who stood near the thrones, hesitated before making the slow trek to her destination. The underlings were notorious for calling her forth, only to turn the tables and torment her.

What games are these fiends up to this time?

She passed by the silver-eyed Verbard and caught a whiff of his fetid port breath.

He rapped her on the behind with his cane, sending a painful jolt through her limbs, and said, "Get moving!"

She shook, and her legs bowed. Though she started to

stumble, she fought to stay upright and lifted her chin as if nothing had happened then made her way to the pedestal of precious stones.

Catten's eyes, burning like two golden coins, locked on hers. "Pick one," he said.

She'd been in the presence of the underlings since they created the pedestal and had a strong understanding of what the mystic mechanism was all about. The stones were used to control the Time Mural.

The beautiful arrangement of colorful gemstones pulsated with inner light, casting a rainbow of colors on her face. She stretched her fingers over the stones and could feel arcane power caressing her bones.

She lifted her stare to Catten, who returned an approving nod.

Here goes. He'll probably burn my fingers off.

A square-cut amethyst, one of many in the grid of stones, caught her eye. She slowly picked it up. Its touch warmed her hand. She tightened her fist around it and started to ask, "Now what?" but bit her tongue.

"Face the Time Mural," Catten ordered.

Image after image flashed in the Time Mural. Some barely lasted a moment, others a second or two, before shifting to another picture. She saw places all over the world, many she recognized and others she didn't. The jagged black peaks of Dark Mountain appeared. The windswept grasses of Westerlund were in full view. Valley

Shire was a beautiful land with forests laden with spectacular trees that were one of a kind. Each and every picture was as captivating as the last, and some stole her breath away.

Catten floated along one side and Verbard along the other, pinning her between their shoulders.

"We want you to try something, elf woman. When you see an image you feel strongly about, use your connection with your stone, and hold that image," Catten said.

Tatiana swallowed. She'd watched some other wizards from the watch attempt the same challenge, only to have their minds turn to goo as drool spilled from their lips. Her time had come. It could be her death.

She nodded and said, "As you wish, Lord Catten."

"Good." Catten drifted back behind to the pedestal and held his hands over the stones. "We'll be trying something different this time. During my meditations, I had an epiphany."

"Is that so, brother?" Verbard asked as he spun and faced him. "When were you going to share this information with me?"

Catten started rearranging the stones in the pedestal. "I was curious to see if you would figure it out yourself. I'm surprised you didn't. Certainly, you recall the time when we summoned a demon from another world to dispatch of one of our fiercest foes?"

"Ah." Verbard's silver eyes brightened. He scratched his

cheek with his pointed black fingernail. "That does bring back memories. A painful reminder of the past." He caught Tatiana looking at him out of the corner of her eyes and poked her ribs with Gossamer's cane, sending a jolt through her. "Stop staring!"

"Guh!" she gasped, dropping the gemstone and falling to the floor. The amethyst bounced off the floor and stopped a few feet from the Time Mural.

"Brother, will you stop tormenting the elf woman? We are conducting an experiment, and she'll need all of her fortitude to survive." Catten sighed. "Elf woman, fetch the stone. Hurry!"

She picked herself up, gritting her teeth. Her body spasmed, and she fought through the painful sensation coursing through her limbs and picked up the stone. Staring into the ever-changing abyss of images, she allowed a gentle bend in her knees. There was still plenty of elf left in her. *I should jump and end this.*

"Elf woman," Catten said, "don't stand so close. You might be tempted to do something stupid."

Verbard had crept up on her and pressed the end of the cane into her back. "And that would force me to blast you into little pieces. You don't want to wind up like so many other members of your pathetic Wizard Watch, do you?"

"Of course not, Lord Verbard. Lord Catten." She inhaled deeply. "I hope to fare far better than them."

"Good." Verbard rapped her on the head with the silver ball handle of his cane. "Now, let's see how much energy your grey matter can hold."

26

TATIANA GRIPPED the gemstone and stood in front of the ominous archway, which was so large that it dwarfed her. Image after image flashed, revealing living things of all sorts and dark and beautiful places.

The enchanted gemstone pulsated in her palm. Like the Star of Light she'd once possessed and Catten now carried, she summoned its magic and became one with it. It was part of her sorcery, which the Wizard Watch taught her, and the mastery of other magical objects.

Along the rim of the Time Mural's archway, the other gemstones brightened with their own majestic light. The array of colors flashed and flickered, bathing the chamber in pools of swirling light.

"Good, good," Catten uttered. "Bond with the portal. Use your stone and bend it to your will!"

Tatiana had seen others attempt to freeze the time portal before, only to witness their quick and ugly demise. They were never the same afterward. Like her, they hadn't had a choice. She lifted the stone, called forth the wizardry, and channeled it through her. Power that felt hot as coals coursed through her blood.

An image of a green pond surrounded by tall willow trees appeared in the mural. She'd spent her time there as a child. A wave of strong memories surfaced in her mind— her first kiss; the use of magic; an untimely death.

Lock it!

Matching amethysts mounted in the archway burned brighter than the other stones. Rays of light burst forth from the stones and joined with the stone in her hand.

Tatiana's eyes were as wide as saucers, and her mouth hung open. The vision of the pond didn't change. It remained in place.

"Hold it, elf woman. Hold it!" Catten demanded.

Verbard drifted closer to the Time Mural. He passed his cane through the amethyst's light and gave a victorious grin.

A dull pain started in her mind and began to quickly build. Tatiana's arm started to tremble. It carried into her body.

"Hold it! Hold it!" Catten shouted.

Tatiana focused on the image. It was a place that she

would not let go—a place she knew strongly. *I won't let go! I'll hold it!*

A great pressure built in her mind and became more intense by the moment. The amethyst burned like a bright star in her hand. The image in the Time Mural began to warp and twist.

"A little longer!" Catten cried. "A little longer!"

Tatiana screamed, and her knees buckled. She collapsed to the ground, and the smoking amethyst rolled free of her blistered fingers. Shaking like a leaf, she lay on the ground, lips sputtering and tears running from her eyes.

Verbard hovered over her, pointed the cane at her, and asked, "Should I put her out of her misery?"

"No." Catten floated alongside his brother and glared down at her. "She fared far better than the others. She held the Time Mural in place at length. Unprecedented."

"I suppose if she can still fetch port, she can be serviceable." Verbard poked her with his cane. "Can you crawl, elf woman?"

Tatiana's teeth clattered. She managed a feeble nod.

"Crawl, then!" Verbard commanded.

"Why don't you lend her a hand, brother?" Catten suggested.

"I'm not touching that hideous thing. Where's an urchling when you need one? I never would have imagined I'd miss my physically maligned brethren." Verbard made a rolling gesture with his cane.

Tatiana tumbled over the floor and bumped into the bases of the underlings' thrones.

"I'll give you a brief amount of time to prove you can pour my port. If you can't do it in the time I've allotted, I'll feed you to..." Verbard looked about. "Well, some sort of abominable creature."

"Will you quit trolling the elf woman, brother? We have more important matters to attend to. Our little experiment was nothing short of a success." Catten waved his brother to the pedestal. "Come. See."

Verbard joined him. The hawk-nosed men leaned over the pedestal and started speaking to each other in another language that sounded like the chittering of birds. Catten spoke and pointed at the stones, while Verbard rubbed his chin and nodded.

Tatiana rubbed her shivering shoulders and tried to shake the burning fog from her mind. She'd never felt such raw power like what she'd felt from the Time Mural. She'd held its might in her grasp for a moment, and it hadn't killed her. It fed her.

The underlings paid her no mind as their chittering conversation began to heat up. They'd spoken often in their underling language before, and she'd picked up bits and pieces of it.

I've never heard them so excited. They must be getting close.

She crawled over to a small serving table and picked up the crystal bottle of port. Her bony arms continued to tremble, and she spilled port on the ground.

"Stop wasting it, or I'll waste you!" Verbard said.

"Will you ignore her? She's not harming anything," Catten said. "Pay attention!"

"She's harming my port. It's the only thing worth having in this world," Verbard replied as he turned his back on her.

Tatiana continued to pour. Her teeth no longer clattered, nor did her arm tremble. What little strength she had returned to her tingling limbs.

Ah, I'm still serviceable, rodents—more serviceable than I'm going to let on.

She finished filling the goblet and wiped the spilled port away from the goblet's rim. With a painful groan, she rose. Keeping her head tilted slightly to one side, she made the trek across the room toward the underlings.

"Your port, Lord Verbard, as requested," she said with a thick tongue.

Verbard floated around in a half circle and faced her with glaring eyes. "Did you interrupt our conversation, elf woman?"

"But Lord Ver—"

With a stroke of his cane, Verbard sent Tatiana sailing across the chamber and slamming into the wall. "I said you need to pour it, not serve it!"

"Stay focused on the task at hand, brother," Catten demanded.

Verbard looked at the shattered crystal on the floor and seethed. "She spilled my port. She's going to have to pay for it."

27

RUINS OF THANNIS

THE GROUP of undead people looked at Grey Cloak like a rock they'd seen a thousand times before and shuffled on.

He held his hand over his chest, and his heart thumped underneath his fingers. *Zooks.*

Grey Cloak walked backward toward the other side of the underwater lake where he'd come from. He didn't take his eyes off the undead as he did so and watched with avid curiosity as the undead trove of people gathered at a break in a knee-high stone wall and started filling it in with stones.

They're working, but why? How?

It didn't make sense that the mindless, deteriorating men and women were working as if they were living. Perhaps they only knew the life that once was.

Maybe Dalsay will understand what is going on.

He hurried up the slope to where his friends were gathered. All of them were glaring at him, either with their arms crossed or brows knitted.

"A welcome back would be nice," he said.

Zora stepped on his toe. "Don't do that again."

"Ow. Zooks, Zora, it's better that I risk my neck than the rest of you."

"What did you discover?" Gorva asked.

"I'll tell you what I discovered. A group of the undead looked right through me and kept going. Nearly scared me out of my boots. That's what I discovered." He gave a nervous chuckle. "I don't think they care that we're here. I don't think they care about anything."

Dalsay intervened and said, "That's because they are zombies. They don't have the ability to care about anything or anyone, living or dead."

"They were walking around like normal people, except they smell like they haven't bathed in a thousand years, and parts of their limbs had fallen off," Grey Cloak said. "But much of their clothing had held up well."

"Creepy," Dyphestive uttered. He ventured forward. "I want to go see them."

"Bear in mind that all who have entered have not come out," Dalsay warned. "We must proceed with great caution. I sense a great evil lurking within, luring us into a trap. Follow me and stay close."

The company made the short trek to the border of Thannis and entered the fallen city.

Zombies wandered the streets and didn't pay them any notice.

Zora wrapped her arms around Grey Cloak's and whispered, "My skin is crawling. Don't they see us?"

"I guess, but perhaps they don't care, or perhaps we're dead already."

"Don't say that." Zora's nose twitched. "They smell awful."

"Uh-huh," Grey Cloak replied as he took a closer look at his surroundings. It appeared that many fallen buildings had been rebuilt. Several structures made from blocks of differently shaped and sized stones towered. The buildings' lines were askew in most places, but somehow the leaning fortifications stood.

"How in the world is that standing?" Zora asked. Then she crushed Grey Cloak's arm. "Eek!"

A herd of tarantulas the size of large hounds scurried across the road, up the buildings, and over the rooftops and vanished.

"Those spiders are huge. I've never seen them so big," Zora said.

"It's a good thing you weren't with us on Prisoner Island," Grey Cloak said.

"Why? Were there giant spiders?"

He nodded. "Big enough to ride. So, Dalsay, should we

split up and look for the figurine? I don't think the zombies will have a problem with us poking around."

Dalsay stood with his arms by his sides and his eyes closed.

Dyphestive was on the other side of the wizard, looking right through him. "I think he's concentrating." He passed his hand through Dalsay's neck. "Huh, that made the hair on my arms stand up. Come over here and do this, Grey." He continued to pass his hand through Dalsay.

Leena grabbed his hand and pulled it away.

"Never mind," Dyphestive said.

Dalsay opened his eyes, surveyed the group, and said, "There is strong magic running through the veins of this city. We need to find its source, and that is where we will find our answers."

"I hope you aren't sensing more giant spiders," Zora said with a shiver.

"You mean a spider sense?" Grey Cloak quipped.

"I like the sound of that," Zora said. "Seeing spiders before they creep up on you. Or I could hunt them down and squish them."

"Why would you want to do that?" Gorva asked. "Spiders eat all the bad bugs like mosquitos and those annoying moths."

"I don't like spiders, and I'm free to dislike as I please," Zora replied.

Grey Cloak's mind wandered off. *If I was here before,*

where would I have put the figurine? There are thousands of places to hide it. And did I bring it here? Why would I do that? Did I do that to hide it, or did I do it so that only I could find it? He smirked. *My, I'm a complex elf. It's good to be me. Nothing like excitement mixed with mystery.*

Zora nudged him. "What are you smiling about?"

He twirled his index finger around his ear and said, "Only entertaining some thoughts. Dalsay, I think we should split up into two groups. You lead one, and I'll lead the other."

"We should stay together," Dalsay said. "Splitting up now would be foolish against these numbers."

Grey Cloak touched his chest and said, "If I hid the figurine here, more than likely, I'll be the one to find it. And I don't think marching into the heart of danger is the best idea."

"Haven't you made enough foolish decisions?" Dalsay retorted. "You need to learn to trust others."

He stood nose to nose with Dalsay and replied, "Watch what you say, wizard!"

Dyphestive interrupted them both and said, "Friends, I'd like to draw your attention to something."

Grey Cloak's ears were heated. "What?"

Dyphestive pointed down the street.

A mass of zombie soldiers in full armor marched straight toward the company.

"Huh," Grey Cloak said. "This might be a problem."

28

THE ARMORED ZOMBIES appeared from all directions. They wore tarnished bronze helmets with purple plumes, matching bronze breastplates, and leggings with thigh and shin guards that rattled when they walked. They took determined shuffling steps, one step after the other. The sinew and skin of their limbs hung from the bone in many places. Their slack jaws were portals to small abysses.

Jakoby drew his sword, and Dyphestive cocked the iron sword over his shoulder.

"No!" Dalsay said. "Lower your weapons. So long as their weapons are not drawn, neither should yours be."

"Are you mad?" Jakoby asked. "Those things will rip us apart."

"We need to run," Grey Cloak said, but he didn't see an avenue for escape. The streets and alleys filled slowly with zombie soldiers. He pulled both of his blades halfway out of their sheaths. "And now, while we can still carve a path through them."

"Agreed," Gorva said.

"I told you not to come here, but you insisted," Dalsay replied. "There is no choice but to see it through. This is the path you have chosen."

"What do we do, Grey?" Dyphestive asked.

He glared at Dalsay and stuffed his swords back in their sheaths with a click. "You'd better be right about this, wizard."

The zombie soldiers were six deep when they surrounded them. With Talon crammed between their ranks, they marched deeper into the city.

"Phew!" Jakoby said. "And I thought long marches with the Monarch Knights smelled bad. These things reek, but they are wearing the finest crafted armor I ever saw."

Dyphestive agreed. "Look at the pommels of their swords. Those handles are pearl. Zombies or no, they are worth a fortune."

They couldn't have been more right. The zombies might be deteriorating, but their armor had held up very well. Even their sword belts and scabbards glimmered with precious stones.

Zora held onto Grey Cloak with one arm and covered her nose with the other. "This stinks."

"Literally."

Gorva couldn't hide her disgust and asked, "How do the dead live? It's not natural."

"Only the strongest and darkest magic can reanimate the dead. They are not living things, as we know one another, but instead, they are flesh golems given temporary life by another being or beings," Dalsay said. "I admit that I am very eager to meet whoever or whatever has executed this massive incantation."

"I have a feeling you're going to learn the answer to that question soon enough," Grey Cloak said as they turned down another block.

At the end of the road was a massive square cathedral with tall ivory towers topped with golden spires on the corners. A wide stone staircase led into the towering double doors, which opened from the inside. The zombie soldiers lined up along both sides of the staircase, forming a passage that led inside.

Grey Cloak moved to the front, beside Dalsay and Dyphestive. The three of them were the first to cross the threshold, and the doors immediately closed behind them, sealing their friends outside.

Dyphestive spun around, dropped his sword, grabbed the door handles, and started to pull.

The others pounded on the door from the other side. Their voices were muted.

"Urrrgh!" Dyphestive moaned as he set his foot against

one door and pulled the iron handle of the other. "It won't budge."

"Use more leg!" Grey Cloak demanded.

Knots of sinewy muscle bulged in Dyphestive's huge arms. His cheeks turned bloodred.

Pop! The handle came off the door, and Dyphestive went flying backward. He landed on his behind and rolled flat on his back. He held up the long twisted iron handle and said, "Not the outcome I was hoping for."

"Who dares enter my temple and defile my property?"

The haunting voice came from the opposite end of the temple. Down the aisle, which was filled with wooden pews over one hundred rows deep, a lone figure waited in the shadows created by torches bracketed on the walls and huge metal chandeliers that burned with flickering green flames.

Dyphestive stood and chucked the handle aside. "We do."

"Let me do the talking," Dalsay demanded.

"Come forward, interlopers," the figure said.

Grey Cloak and Dyphestive fell in step behind Dalsay.

"Did that sound like a woman to you? It did to me," Grey Cloak said.

"I think you're right," Dyphestive replied.

"In that case, I should do the talking. Women like me better," Grey Cloak whispered back.

"They do not. They like me as well as you."

"First off, they don't, and second, you are spoken for."

"Will you stop saying that? I'm not spoken for. Leena and I are only friends."

Grey Cloak smirked. "Tell her that."

"Silence!" The figure lingered inside the swirling black fog on the stage. The fog began to dissipate, revealing a tall, ugly woman with burning ice-blue eyes and a crown of gold. Long strands of white hair hung over her bony shoulders, and skin had rotted off her face. She wore drab, frayed, and moth-eaten robes, and her hands and fingers were all bone. She had no lips. "I am Mortis, Queen of Thannis."

Grey Cloak slipped behind Dyphestive, pushed him in the back, and said, "You can have her."

Dyphestive shook his head. "No, you can have her. I insist."

"At least this one has a tongue that works." Grey Cloak kept pushing. "Think about the benefits. She can probably whistle and hum. Wouldn't that be nice?"

"Silence!"

A shock wave knocked Grey Cloak and Dyphestive off their feet.

Grey Cloak stuck his fingers in his ringing ears, patted his brother's back, and said, "Maybe you should stick with Leena."

29

QUEEN MORTIS LAUNCHED into a tirade about the history of Thannis, including its triumphs and failures. "Our armies never lost in battle. Streams of silver filled our coffers. No heights could not be reached. Sacrifices cost the lives of the living. No man ever touched a hair on my head."

"Dalsay, what is she?" Grey Cloak asked in a low voice.

"She is a lich, an omnipotent undead creature who carries astounding power. Shh, stay silent, and we may learn something."

"You listen all you want. I'm going to take a look around." He nudged his brother. "Let's go."

"But I want to hear what she has to say. It's interesting," Dyphestive said.

"Lap it up, then. I'll be about."

Dyphestive groaned. "Fine, I'll go. It's not as if I can't still listen."

"Precisely."

For some reason, Mortis spoke at length without the slightest concern for what they were doing. So long as they didn't interrupt her speech, the lich appeared content to let them do what they would. Grey Cloak navigated through the pews, searching for anything that might be helpful.

Dyphestive searched another row beside him and asked, "What are we looking for?"

"The figurine. I could have put it anywhere, knowing me." He ran his hand underneath the benches and peeked under each and every one of them.

All the while, Mortis continued talking.

"The world swallowed our city, but it didn't ingest our spirit," she said. "We are more than tile and stone. More than flesh and bone. We live forever."

"Her speech is lasting forever," Dyphestive said.

"Apparently, she doesn't have anyone to talk to and has centuries of catching up to do," Grey Cloak replied. "Listen, you search the pews on the other side. I'm going to take my chances on the stage."

"Don't get too close her... or it," Dyphestive said.

While Dalsay held audience with Mortis, Grey Cloak hurried onto the temple stage and began to look around. There were tables with serving platters covered in dust and dirt. Several high-backed wooden chairs with torn velvet cushions were lined up against the wall in the back. But in the middle of the stage, several feet away from Mortis's back, was an altar chiseled out of pure jade and covered in bloodstains.

Grey Cloak's stomach turned at the thought of the sacrifices that must have been made in the name of evil. Resting on the slab was a foot-long dagger with a very curious design. The gilding around the handle was pure gold, and an oversized emerald was fastened into the bottom of the handle by tiny claws. The blade itself was the most unique design Grey Cloak had ever beheld. It had four blades in a conical shape that came to a point at the top. The purpose of the design was obvious. To stop the bleeding from a puncture wound from that dagger would be nearly impossible.

Murderers.

His hand hovered over the dagger as he stared at the talking lich's back.

I could pick it up and put an end to her, but she's already dead. Zooks. How do you kill someone that's dead?

Something about the dagger held his gaze. It called out to him in a sinister velvety voice, *"Take me in hand. I am your friend. I will show you what you need."*

Wide-eyed and heart pounding, Grey Cloak lowered his hand over the handle. His fingers started to close on the grip.

A strong hand seized his wrist. He tried to twist out of it.

"Grey Cloak, what are you doing?" Dyphestive asked. "Don't touch that instrument of evil. It's cursed."

He blinked and stared back at his brother. "How... how do you know that?"

Dyphestive shrugged. "I don't know how, but I do. Did you find anything else?"

He gave a feeble nod, but Mortis's tirade caught his attention.

Her head twisted over her shoulders and faced them. "Whoever enters Thannis stays in Thannis. You are one of us now. Destined to join my growing army. We vow to return to the surface and take over a world that is rightfully ours." Her burning blue eyes fastened on the dagger. "Use it. End your life. The life of your companions. In death, there is no worry. There is no pain. There is only victory."

An uncomfortable silence followed as Mortis stood before them without saying a word.

Grey Cloak wasn't shy about breaking the silence. "You aren't going to kill us outright?"

Mortis offered a wide smile of missing teeth and said, "No, you will be dead soon enough. There is no food or water you can drink. It's only a small matter of time before you are at each other's throats." She tapped her bony fingers together. *Click. Click. Click.* "And I will delight in your misery."

Grey Cloak raised a finger. "But to be clear, you aren't going to kill us or try to kill us now?"

"Unless you do something foolish, the pleasures Thannis has to offer are yours to enjoy," Mortis said.

"Can you define 'something foolish'?"

"Don't try to leave. My army will slay you. Don't raid the coffers. It will seal your doom. Century after century, treasure hunters seek out the riches of Thannis, only to find their doom. They are soldiers in my army now. Soon, so will the rest of you be."

"Great! I wanted to make sure there wasn't any misunderstanding. Can we leave now?"

"The temple, yes. The city, no."

The front doors to the cathedral opened wide.

Not a single soul stood in the entrance.

"Goy! Where'd our friends go?" Dyphestive demanded.

Mortis laughed.

30

RAZOR

OVER ONE THOUSAND feet above Thannis, a drizzling rain started coming down from the cloudy daylight sky. The horses whinnied and nickered as a stiff breeze picked up and bowed the smaller surrounding trees.

The green leaves turned upside down, and Reginald the Razor muttered, "Great, a storm is coming."

With one eye on the sky, he watched a flock of geese soar overhead toward the southwest.

"I wouldn't mind some cooked goose about now."

One of the bigger horses, the one that Dyphestive rode, let out a loud snort and stomped his hooves.

"Hold your horses," Reginald said in his rugged voice. He shook his head. "That must have sounded stupid."

He made his way over to Cliff the mule and prepared a feed bag. "They're down there having all the fun, while I'm up here playing with the animals. Lucky me." He fastened the feed bag on Dyphestive's horse, scratched it behind the ears, and said, "There, that should keep you quiet."

A couple of other horses snorted and wiggled their necks in his direction.

"You'll have to wait." He pointed at the river. "Go get a drink from the river if you're thirsty." He walked to the end of the overlook and watched the white mist of the waterfall plummet into the water of the Outer Ring. Over one hundred feet below, the falls cascaded in front of the spot where his friends had vanished. "I should have gone."

Razor might not have been a fan of climbing, but he was no fan of missing out on a fight either. Staying behind with the horses felt cowardly. He tested the rope that hung over the overlook and peered over again. It was a long plunge if he fell into the watery gorge that formed the Outer Ring. He let go of the rope and said, "They're probably on their way back. In the meantime..." He drew two daggers that were sheathed below his ribs on both sides and spun them in his hands then stuffed them back in their sleeves.

Razor carried twelve blades at all times, at least where permissible. Twelve was his number of fortune, and he saw to it that he carried it with him, in one way or the other, preferably in the form of edged weapons, at all times. Two long swords were crisscrossed over his back. A pair of short swords dressed his hips. Below his black leather armor were two daggers. Two more daggers were strapped to his thighs, matched by two more strapped to his shins above his boots. Behind his back was another pair of daggers hooked into his belt, making twelve in all.

He closed his eyes and took a deep breath. One by one, he drew each blade, stabbed an unseen opponent, and sheathed the weapon again. He'd practiced the same routine over a thousand times in his lifetime, pressing to be quicker every time.

New sweat mixed with the light drizzle, and he launched into another routine.

Razor pulled two swords from behind his back.

Jab, step, slice. Jab, step, chop.

He sheathed them again then exercised the same routine with each pair of blades while creating different combinations.

Razor's action grew into a blur of steel. He finished his routine, leaving a long sword in his right hand and a short sword in his left. A monarch butterfly with burnt-orange wings floated by. He chased it. The butterfly's erratic flight pattern made it a perfect target for practice.

His short sword flashed. He shaved one wing off the butterfly. Then he sliced through its body before it hit the ground.

He wiped the sweat from his brow with his forearm, sheathed his blades, and grabbed a skin of water that hung from his horse. He chugged the water in big gulps, then something caught his eye.

"What do we have here?" he asked as he corked the waterskin.

Far away on the trail that ran along the base of the Iron Hills, a group of riders approached. They were only the size of ants from that distance, and they disappeared underneath the next rise, only to reappear again a few minutes later, growing in size.

Razor wiped his mouth and put the waterskin away. Talon's camp was far off the beaten path. There wasn't anywhere to go but over the cliff, which made for an unlikely journey.

"Whoever is coming is coming for a reason." He grabbed the rope and spooled it over his shoulder, then he tossed it aside in the high grasses near the rocky base of the hills. He flexed his fingers. "So much for boredom."

The clouds darkened. A light rumble of thunder was accompanied by flashes of lightning. The drizzle became a steady rain, obscuring Razor's vision.

He grabbed a blanket, covered himself, and found a spot in the hills to hide that gave him full view of the trail.

Look at me, hiding in the bushes like a coward. At least there isn't anyone around to see.

Only one rise was left on the trail between them and the river's drop-off. The small group had disappeared from view and hadn't appeared again.

Razor ran through scenarios of what might be coming.

Could be bandits. I could handle them.

It might be soldiers. Again, I could handle them.

There is no telling who might be tracking us.

Maybe it's allies—not likely but possible. I could definitely handle them. Perhaps it's a group of beautiful women seeking my hand in marriage. Lucky them. Here I am.

Through the rain, he saw four riders come into view over the final rise. They came forward at a slow gait, on the backs of the biggest horses he'd ever seen. They were no more than one hundred yards away, but the long strides of the beasts moved them faster than common horses would.

With no more than fifty yards between them, Razor got his first good look at all of them. Big rangy men rode tall in their saddles. Behind the tallest horse was a bald woman with an eye patch covering her left eye.

Instead of horses, they rode on extraordinary beasts that were built like horses but covered in scales and with the heads and horns of dragons.

Razor tightened his blanket over his shoulders. Nearby, the horses' snorts and nervous nickers grew louder. He swallowed the lump building in his throat and said under his breath, "Bust my acorns, those are Doom Riders."

31

THE DOOM RIDERS wandered into camp on the clawed feet of their gourns. Smoke huffed out of the gourns' nostrils and mouths. Like horses, they had hooves on their back legs, but their front feet were like lion paws with sharp claws that dug into the soft dirt of the riverbank.

Two of the riders swung their legs out of their saddles and dropped to the ground. Both of them wore worn, blackened leather armor that was fashioned like dragon scales. One of them wore a dyed-red leather mask resembling a skull. The other man's mask was dyed blue.

Like Razor, both men had long swords crisscrossed across their backs. They eased their way through the camp, checking the horses and the gear that they carried.

That left the other two riders sitting tall in their

saddles, observing. The man wore a green mask, and red hair spilled from underneath it and touched his shoulders.

The bald woman wore an eye patch instead of a mask. She was armored the same as the others but wore a chain mail sleeve on her left arm. Unlike the men, she wore her sword belt on her hip, and over her back was a crossbow unlike any crossbow Razor had ever seen. It had bolts loaded into a cylinder.

Razor's jaw clenched. He'd been in several conversations about the group before but had never seen them in person.

Red is Scar. Blue is Ghost. Green is Shamrok, and that must be Drysis, but I thought she was dead. And here they are, getting into my business. Bloody biscuits. It looks like the day I've been waiting for has come. It's going to be a battle royale.

Wrapped in a wet blanket, Razor wandered out of his hiding spot in the bushes.

The Doom Riders, gourns included, turned and faced him.

"Can I help you with something?" he asked.

Drysis spoke in a strong but brittle voice, her lone black pupil searching his face. "Is this your camp?"

He faked a cough and said, "It is."

"You have a lot of horses and a lot of gear for one man," she said.

"That's my business."

The other three Doom Riders began to spread out and surround him.

"Ah, I see. You are bandits come to rob me."

Drysis shook her head. "We are not bandits. We are a search party, looking for... old friends. Perhaps you have seen them."

"I've seen a lot of things in my life but never old friends. I like the young ones."

"What is your name?" she asked.

"Reginald." He had to bite his tongue to keep from adding the Razor part, though it killed him not to do so.

"Reginald, do I appear to be someone you can take for a fool?"

He studied her hard jawline and the blue veins on her pasty face. "I'm not sure what I take you for. Any of you. I see scary masks and scary horses, and I can't help but wonder what festival I missed out on."

Scar said, "The only thing missing is going to be your head if you don't start talking."

"Is that so?" Razor asked as he bought time and continued to size them up. All of them were well-knit, above average in size and build, with eyes as hard as iron. "Don't get too cocky. You see, whoever you are looking for, well, I killed them. Chopped them down and pitched them into the ring. Their horses and gear are mine now."

"And you accomplished this feat all by yourself?" Drysis asked.

"I did. My skills are notorious in these hills. They call me the Lone Blade." He took a bow.

Scar and Shamrok broke out in gruff laughter.

"Drysis, let us finish off the mule thief," Scar suggested. "He's only wasting our time."

"I believe it's the other way around. You interrupted my day. I didn't interfere with yours," he said.

"Where are the others?" Drysis demanded.

"I told you. Their bodies float on the waters of the Outer Ring."

Drysis narrowed her eye on him and said, "I tire of this. Bring him to me."

Razor dropped his blanket and drew a long sword and a short sword in the wink of an eye.

Scar's head tilted, and he said, "Lords of Steel, how many blades are you carrying, mate?"

"I carry twelve. Do you think you can handle them?"

Shamrok chuckled and said to Scar, "It sounds like someone is overcompensating for something. A real fighter only needs one."

Razor spun his swords on his wrists and said, "We'll see about that."

Shamrok started to dismount.

Drysis lifted a hand and said, "No, stay put."

"You can't see me grinning under this mask, but I have a beautiful smile all over my face," Scar said. He reached behind his back and drew both of his long blades. "This is going to be a dance to remember."

Drysis shook her head at Scar. "No, not you either." She turned her frosty gaze to another Doom Rider. "Ghost, I'll let you take this cocky little fighter apart. But keep him alive. Once it's over, I'll have questions."

32

THE RUINS OF THANNIS

THE STREETS of Thannis were clear—no zombie soldiers, no aimlessly wandering citizens, and no members of Talon. The town was abandoned.

Grey Cloak jogged down the stairs and asked, "What is the meaning of this? How could they be gone?" He spun around. "All of them are gone?"

"We were in there a long time," Dyphestive stated. "Long enough for them to move on."

"Dalsay, go inside and ask your new friend what happened to our old friends, why don't you?" Grey Cloak said.

"It appears that Mortis has moved on. I don't see her," Dalsay replied.

Grey Cloak picked up a hunk of stone and chucked it across the street. It smacked against a building, bounced, and clattered down the street. "Well, isn't this fantastic? Why in the world would I ever come here in the first place?"

"You can't be certain that you *have* been here. That might have been a lie," Dyphestive said. He walked down the steps with his sword resting on his shoulder. "We'll find them."

"Dalsay, any brilliant ideas?" he asked.

"Obviously, Mortis enjoys playing games. I suggest we separate and look for them. I can travel faster without the two of you, as passage through obstacles won't slow me."

"Well, what are you waiting for, Ghost Man?" Grey Cloak shooed him away. "Get going."

"Aaaiiieee!"

The scream echoed down the street.

"That was Zora! I'd know that scream from anywhere!" Grey Cloak started running toward the source of the sound. "Come on!"

When he was five strides into the run, the air whistled by his ears, and his cloak flapped behind his back. He heard another high-pitched scream.

"Aaaiiieee!"

The sound echoed from another direction. He skidded to a halt and scanned the surrounding buildings.

Dyphestive caught up with him and said, "Horseshoes, you're as fast as a jackrabbit."

"I'm faster than that. Be silent."

Zora's scream faded into the distance.

"I don't have any sense of direction of where that sound came from," Grey Cloak said. "It sounded like it came from over there." He pointed down an alley. "Then it came from down that way." He pointed in the direction Dyphestive had come from. "Zora!"

The sound of his voice carried down the streets and echoed back to him a moment later.

"Zooks, this is madness!"

Dyphestive put a hand on Grey Cloak's shoulder. "We'll find her." He closed his eyes. "We only need to concentrate."

Grey Cloak trusted his eyes and ears. The only thing he heard was his own heart beating.

Then came another distressed scream. It came from all directions, echoed, and faded away once more.

He slowly shook his head.

If I can't trust my ears, I'll have to trust my other senses.

His nostrils flared, and he took in a deep draw of air.

The rotting city carried a musty scent like garbage after the rain. The suffocating smell stayed with you everywhere you went. The only thing worse was the reek of the zombies.

"Aaaiiieee!"

Grey Cloak's nose twitched.

"I wish I had Streak. Where is my dragon when I need

him? He'd lick her scent right up, but my tongue's not going to touch this pavement."

Dyphestive took in short bursts of air through his nostrils. His nose crinkled, and he asked, "Doesn't Zora wash with lavender?"

"Come to think of it, yes." Grey Cloak's nose twitched like a bunny's. Elated, he said, "I smell it. Ew, and not only that."

"Sorry," Dyphestive said with a guilty look.

"That was you? Oh, that's awful. I'd forgotten how rotten you could be."

"My stinks are worse when I'm excited. It happens." Dyphestive took off down the street. "Hurry while her scent is still strong."

Grey Cloak followed Dyphestive with Zora's scent lingering in his nose. When he'd trained at Hidemark with the beautiful, honey-haired elven sisters, Mayzie and Stayzie, they conducted survival tests with him in the wild. They told him being a natural gave him heightened senses beyond those of ordinary men. He was taught to walk blind through jungle terrain and learn to rely on his other senses. The problem was that he'd learned to rely more on the Cloak of Legends more than his own instincts.

"Aaaiiieee!"

Zora's scream might have been echoing from all directions, but it was getting louder.

"This way!" Dyphestive said.

They raced down an alley and angled into a wider street. They sniffed again.

"Aaaiiieee!"

Grey Cloak pointed. "There!"

On the opposite end of the road, two blocks down, Zora dashed across the street with a pack of dog-sized spiders on her tail.

He took off at full speed and closed the distance on the alley she'd vanished into in a few seconds. Three spiders blocked his entrance. Zora was trapped in a dead end with spiders closing in.

"Help!" she shouted.

Without slowing, Grey Cloak leaped over the web-spitting spiders and drew his blades. He landed on the back of an ugly tarantula and gored its body with steel. "Hang on, Zora! I'm coming!"

"Hurry!" she cried. Her dagger flashed downward, butchering the face of a tarantula. "I can't hold them off!"

The spiders backed her against the wall and began shooting webbing. A blast of gooey spider silk pinned her dagger to her body. She groaned.

Grey Cloak sliced off the legs of one spider and buried his blade in the side of another. He chopped and hacked at anything that moved. Spiders collapsed in heaps of their own goo.

More spiders appeared from above. They came from

the roof and climbed down the wall, shooting parachutes of webbing that came down like a slow rain.

"That's a problem." Grey Cloak carved a path through two spiders in an effort to evade the webbing dropping over his head. A strand of spider silk latched onto his boot and yanked it off. "Dirty acorns!"

"Hurry, Grey Cloak!" Zora was covered in strands of webs. "They're covering me up!"

"Coming!" Grey Cloak chopped a path through the spiders toward Zora until he was elbow deep in spider guts. "Almost there!"

The webbing parachutes covered his head and shoulders, fastening his limbs together so he couldn't move. He was only a few feet from Zora and surrounded by spiders. "Zooks!"

33

DYPHESTIVE PLOWED INTO THE ALLEY, swiping the iron sword from side to side in broad strokes, crying, "Die, insects! Die!"

The iron sword ripped through three spiders at a time, spilling their guts all over the alley.

"Ha! Taste my iron, Eight Eyes!"

The eight-legged fiends let out odd shrieks and propelled their nasty black-haired bodies at Dyphestive.

Glitch! Dyphestive skewered two spiders with his great sword and shoved their wriggling bodies over his shoulder.

Spiders descended the wall, spitting clouds of cottony web at him.

"What's this?" He stabbed them one by one as they came down the wall. "There are so many! I like it!"

"Dyphestive, watch out for their webs!" Grey Cloak

warned. The spiders had half covered him in webs. The more he wiggled, the more he stuck. "They're strong."

A spider came at him with its small mouth of sharp teeth wide open. It aimed for his bare foot.

Grey Cloak pulled his foot back and hopped away then forced his sword through the sticky webs and drilled the spider in the face. "Take that!"

Another spider snuck across the alley and sank its teeth into his ankle.

"Ow!" Grey Cloak called. He thrust his dagger at the creature, but the webbing clinging to his arms stunted his reach. Above, clouds of webs fell all over. "Zooks! Dyphestive, we've got trouble!"

"Grey Cloak!" Zora hollered in a muffled voice. Her face was half-covered in webbing. "Do something!"

"I'm thinking!"

"Think faster! Use your magic or something!"

A flame of a thought brightened in his mind. "Good idea!" He summoned the wizard fire and pushed the force into his blades. The steel glimmered with radiant blue flame. Every strand of webbing it touched peeled away. His limbs were freed, and he sliced right through the sticky strands. He started butchering the spiders again. "That's more like it!"

"Slay them, brother!" Dyphestive hollered. He stomped a spider into goo. Half-covered in sticky strands, his powerful muscles ripped through the webs. The iron sword went up and came down with force, tearing spiders open and splattering their goo.

Grey Cloak fought his way to Zora, sending spiders by the pair to their graves. Using his dagger, he sliced her bonds away. "Stay close to me. We're getting out of here!"

"How? They're everywhere!"

Webs continued to rain down, and spiders scurried down the walls.

"We can take them." He plunged his hot blue steel into another one. He pushed an added charge of wizard fire into the blade. The spider exploded.

"Whoa!" Zora said. "You did that?"

He smirked. "Impressive, isn't it?"

"Well, it was only one. There must still be a score left."

A spider jumped off the wall toward them. Zora covered her head and screeched.

Grey Cloak swung her away and gutted the spider open.

"Get me out of here! I hate spiders!" Zora screamed.

"I'm trying! Dyphestive, make a hole!"

Dyphestive was covered up to his hips in webbing. Spiders attacked him from all directions. He twisted from side to side, arms pumping, sweeping his blade through them one by one. "I'm trying, but I can't move my legs."

Grey Cloak cut through the strands as fast as he could, but the thick webbing piled up all around them. The street became sticky with webbing, and his feet stuck to the ground. "This is a problem. Watch your step, Zora. We need to find a clear path out of here."

Her lips were curled back over her teeth as she searched the ground and said, "It's sticky everywhere."

Grey Cloak stabbed a spider in the side. "There has to be a better way." He gave Zora his sword. "Use this!"

"It's not my style, but fine!" She swung the sword back and forth, keeping spiders at bay. "What are you doing?"

Grey Cloak fished a handful of coins out of his pocket then summoned his wizardry and filled them with wizard fire. "I'm doing this!"

He flung the coins at the spiders and on the ground.

Boom! Boom! Boom! Boom! Boom! The coins exploded, blowing up the spiders and clearing a path to Dyphestive.

"Well done, brother!" Dyphestive roared. The muscles in his neck bulged and strained. "You inspire me! I'll rip though this!" He started tearing out of the cocoon of webs. "Eeeyargh!"

Spiders pounced on him. Their hairy bodies covered his head and shoulders.

"Dyphestive!" Grey Cloak shouted. "I'm coming!"

Leena burst into the alley with her glowing nunchakus spinning with lethal fury. She tore through the webbing like it was made of rose petals, and the spiders practically exploded.

Chok-tum! Chok-tum! Chok-tum! Chok-tum! The crack of

her wood killed them on the spot. They flattened out on the ground and stiffened.

"Tear them apart, Leena!" Dyphestive shouted as he tore out of the cords.

Leena made every spider that came within two feet of her burst open. Her weapons moved with blinding speed. *Chok-tum! Chok-tum! Chok-tum! Chok-tum!*

The alley fell silent. Not a single spider moved. The path to the main street was cleared.

"Lords of the Air, thank the dragons that is over," Zora said as she picked her way through the dead bodies with Grey Cloak's sword gripped in her shaking hands. "Can we get out of here, please?"

A shadow fell over the group at the end of the alley. It was a towering spider the size of Itchee from Prisoner Island. It blocked their exit with its massive body. Its eight eyes burned like coals.

Dyphestive stepped in front of the group. "I'll handle this." He raised his sword and charged. "It's thunder time!"

34

THE GIANT TARANTULA reared on its back four legs and stabbed its pointed front claws at the charging Dyphestive.

The iron sword came down. *Slice!*

The metal sheared through the ends of the spider's front legs, which spit ooze. The sword's tip cut into the spider's open mouth and hung on the bottom row of its teeth. He shoved the sword into the meat of the spider's skull, piercing its small brain.

It gave an inhuman shriek, which was cut short. Its legs flattened out, and it hit the street with a thump.

Dyphestive wrenched his sword free of the spider's body and slung off the gore. Then he turned and faced his friends. "I told you I'd handle it."

"Zora, what happened?" Grey Cloak asked as he led the group through the city.

"The moment you went into the temple, the zombie soldiers departed. The streets cleared. It was the oddest thing," she said. "We planned to wait, but the spiders came."

"There are more spiders?" he asked.

"Oh yes. Too many to fight. We thought it would be safer to split up and divide their force," she said as she rubbed her scarf. "I used the Scarf of Shadows, but those bloody spiders could still see me. I guess eight eyes are better than two."

"Bloody biscuits, they could be anywhere, and we have to find them," Grey Cloak said. "At least the spiders are gone for now."

"They might have a lair," Dyphestive suggested. He walked with his arm hanging on Leena's shoulder, and she had her small arm around his waist. "We only have to find it."

"That's assuming the spiders have them." Grey Cloak's gaze drifted to the distant cave-riddled hills. They reminded him of the dragon kennels in Dark Mountain. Small bodies were still moving along the ledges, and he could hear the faint clamor of hammers and shovels. "That might not be a bad spot to hide."

"They are not there."

They spun around and found themselves face-to-face with Dalsay.

"Where have you been?" Grey Cloak asked.

"Searching for the others," Dalsay said. "And I have found them."

"All of them?" he asked.

"Are they alive?" Zora added.

Dalsay nodded. "At the moment. We must hurry. Follow me." He moved into the old buildings and vanished from sight, leaving Dyphestive scratching his head. Dalsay reappeared a moment later on the porch of an ancient tavern. "I'll stay on the road, but some doors you are going to have to break."

They jogged through the empty alleys and streets, with Dalsay's ghostly form leading the way. Several blocks away, he came to an intersection where four roads met. A knee-high of neatly stacked stones stood in the center of the intersection. Dalsay hovered over a twenty-foot hole in the ground.

"The arachnids took them down there," Dalsay said as he pointed downward.

The four members of Talon leaned over the wall and peered into the darkness.

"It looks like a giant well," Dyphestive said.

Grey Cloak pointed at the stone steps that spiraled down along the well's inner wall. "Since when do wells have staircases?"

Dalsay floated downward and said, "I'll see you at the bottom."

Grey Cloak slung his leg over the wall and asked, "How deep in this world do we have to go? All the way down to the Flaming Fence?"

"If we have to," Dyphestive said.

Zora grabbed Grey Cloak's arm. She shivered like a leaf and said, "Don't go, please." She averted her eyes from the well. "I-I can't go down there with all those spiders. I can't. Stay with me."

He gently laid a hand on hers and said, "You know I must go. They're our friends. It's fine if you stay up here. The zombies won't harm you. Mortis said so."

"Let Dyphestive and Leena go. You stay with me!"

He tucked her damp strands of hair behind her slightly pointed ears and said, "You'll be safe with us. Come and stay close to me."

Zora shook her head.

Grey Cloak shared a desperate look with Dyphestive.

"Time is ticking!" Dalsay hollered from below.

Leena cut between Grey Cloak and Zora and pushed him back with the palm of her hand then put her arm around Zora's waist. She gave Grey Cloak and Dyphestive intense looks, and with her right hand, she beckoned for them to go.

Grey Cloak searched Zora's eyes. She gave him a nod.

"We'll return soon," he promised. "All of us."

He and Dyphestive descended the spiral staircase into an underworld of total blackness. They were greeted at the bottom by Dalsay. His soft illumination revealed a wide sewer tunnel large enough for men to walk through. It smelled of rot and waste.

Dyphestive found a torch bracketed on the wall and pulled it free. He swung it toward Grey Cloak and said, "Hit me."

"Hit you?"

"Use your wizard fire. Light it up."

"Huh, I never thought about using it like that before." He drew forth energy and pushed it into his dagger. The blade glowed blue, and he jabbed the tip of the torch and drew fire. The flame warmed his face. "I don't think I've ever appreciated a flame more than I do now."

"Agreed," Dyphestive said.

Dalsay led the way down the grimy tunnel. They were sandwiched in a pressing darkness that clung to their light. "I almost feel like the blackness here is a living thing."

"Perhaps it is," Dyphestive agreed.

"As if we didn't have enough troubles." Grey Cloak noticed another torch bracketed on the wall. "That's promising."

Dyphestive lit the torch then repeated the process every twenty or thirty steps.

From far ahead, the sound of rushing water echoed.

"Do you hear that?" Dyphestive asked.

"It sounds like a river," Grey Cloak said.

They hurried down the tunnel, racing toward the sound of the water.

The tunnel ended on a ledge that overlooked a wide current of water cutting through the belly of the earth.

Suddenly, a foul breeze whistled into the tunnel and blew all the torches out.

35

"SO MUCH FOR TORCHLIGHT." Dyphestive tossed his torch aside. "At least we have Dalsay's glow."

"And my fire. Pick up your torch. I can still light it," Grey Cloak suggested.

Dyphestive bent over and picked up the torch.

Grey Cloak lit it again with his dagger. "See?"

"I wonder where that breeze came from," Dyphestive said.

"Does it really matter? Will you get us out of here?" Gorva shouted from somewhere in the blackness.

Grey Cloak looked upward. The ceiling of the river chamber was as black as a coal tunnel. There was nothing to be seen above. He called, "Gorva, where are you?"

"Up here!"

"I can't see a thing from here."

"Let me see if I can shed my light on it." Dalsay's feet left the ground, and he floated higher. His body illuminated the outline of a ceiling.

Grey Cloak's upper lip curled. "Ew."

The ceiling was covered in pockets of webbing and dog-sized spiders crawling among the dew-dripping stalactites.

"That's a lot of spiders," Dyphestive commented.

"Over here, wizard!" Gorva hollered again.

Dalsay drifted under the stalactites and stopped below Gorva.

Her body was in a cocoon of webbing and hung from the ceiling by its strands. She wore a frown as deep as a river.

"Don't gawk. Do something!" she said.

"I don't have the means," Dalsay said. "Where is Jakoby?"

Gorva replied, "He was with me, but they took him. He shouted, then his voice was gone." She wiggled in her bonds. "Now, will you get me out of here?"

"Easier said than done," Grey Cloak said under his breath. "Any ideas, brother?"

Dyphestive shook his head. "There are so many webs. How do we get her without sticking? She's trapped."

"Not to mention that the moment we touch a strand, a spider will come running. Probably all of them."

"Let me try something." Dyphestive moved along the ledge that overlooked the river. Webbing coated the walls in several spots. He put the torch fire against the webs and watched them curl away. "My flame and your power should handle the stickiness."

"True, but we still have to climb up there. And fight the spiders. Dalsay, is there anything that you can do aside from nothing?"

"I can watch and advise."

Grey Cloak let out a sarcastic chuckle. "That's great. You've been so very helpful so far."

"At least he provides a light source," Dyphestive said.

"Yes, but we seem to be doing fine without him," Grey Cloak answered, holding his glowing dagger in front of him. He'd never imagined so many webs in his lifetime. "Zora would jump out of her skin if she came down here. It's a good thing she didn't come." He noticed a natural stone bridge that crossed the river and vanished into the darkness on the other side. "Huh, I wonder where that goes."

"I know how we can find out." Dyphestive climbed down the steep bank of stones that led to the river.

Grey Cloak followed him.

"Where are you going?" Gorva shouted. "Get back up here!"

"Dalsay, make yourself useful and stay with her. We're going to take a look at something," Grey Cloak said.

The steeply pitched stone bridge arced over fifty feet of

rushing black water then knifed into another tunnel in the rock and vanished.

Dyphestive dipped his fingers into the water. "Icy."

"Hold your torch over the water," Grey Cloak said.

The torch flames shone through the ebony stream, revealing a shallow depth on the bank that quickly deepened.

"That's quite a current," Grey Cloak said. "Not likely that a creature lurks in the depths of its waters, but keep an eye out. Let's cross."

"Human! Elf! Get back here and free me!" Gorva demanded.

Grey Cloak started across the shoulder-width bridge and said, "We're going for help!"

"Well, you're going the wrong way!"

They made it halfway across the slick bridge and stopped. A foul breeze sent new chills down Grey Cloak's neck. The torch flames flickered.

Dyphestive leaned over Grey Cloak's shoulder and asked, "What are you waiting for?"

"I can't see where the bridge ends. Our light has too small of a radius." He crept forward and said, "Watch your step."

The bridge was as slick as wet river stones, and it descended at a steeper angle. Grey Cloak wore only one boot, and his feet began to slide. The blackness closed in. "Zooks."

A glance over his shoulder revealed Dyphestive with his arms stretched out and balancing with a sword in one hand and the torch in the other. He started to slide.

"Gangway!" Dyphestive hollered.

Grey Cloak turned toward Dyphestive's body. "Stop, you oaf!"

"I can't!"

Grey Cloak lowered his shoulder into Dyphestive's chest and tried marching up the ramp. His feet slipped over each other and kept sliding downward. "Zooks, you are a load!"

Dyphestive's body gained momentum, and the speed of their slide increased. "I told you to watch out."

"Where was I to go? In the water?" Grey Cloak dug his feet into the rock, hoping to find a foothold in the smooth surface. Even his flexible toes couldn't find purchase.

Down they went, into the darkness waiting to swallow them.

They crashed to the ground, with Dyphestive landing on top.

"Will you get off me?" Grey Cloak asked.

"Sorry." Dyphestive rolled over and lifted his torch. They sat on a rocky bank. "Huh, this side is no different from the other."

Grey Cloak tugged his boot off and slung it down the bank. "I don't know why I even bother to wear boots. They're so restricting."

"You wear them because you don't want to cut your feet on the rocks."

"Impossible when they are that smooth." He started climbing up the riverbank.

"What's going on down there?" Gorva hollered.

"Nothing!" he shouted back.

"Watch out!" she warned.

Grey Cloak turned. "What is it?" He expected to see spiders dropping out of their nests, but there was nothing.

Dyphestive rose then bent over and picked up his sword. A wave washed over his feet, and a white crab the size of a horse with a luminous shell burst out of the water and clamped its huge pincer down on his ankle.

"Eeeargh!"

36

DYPHESTIVE RAISED the iron sword over his head and brought it down on the head of the crab. *Snap!* The iron sword's blade snapped off at the hilt.

"Horseshoes!" he shouted.

The white crab's legs dug into the rock, and it began towing Dyphestive into the icy water of the rushing river.

Dyphestive clawed at the rocks and fastened his strong fingers in a stony groove. "Grey Cloak, some help would be nice!"

Grey Cloak battled the giant crab with sword and dagger. "I *am* helping, I think." He stabbed at the crustacean's free pincer, which jabbed and snipped at him like a striking snake. "That thing is fast!"

"And strong! It broke my sword," Dyphestive said as he held on to the rocks for dear life. "It's pulling my leg off!"

"Hold on!" Grey Cloak turned up his power and unleashed his speed. He struck the crab's attacking claw in a flurry of burning blue steel. Chips of shell and small hunks of flesh started to fly. A quick strike from his sword sliced the smaller snapping bottom pincer off. "Yah! That's progress! Only a hundred more strikes, and you should be free!"

"A hundred more, and we'll both be dead!" Dyphestive pointed toward the river. "Look!"

Several more white crabs crawled under the water toward them.

"That might be a problem," Grey Cloak said.

Dyphestive groaned. His body slid closer to the river. He clung to the rock by the tips of his fingers. "I'm losing my grip. Hurry!"

The crab used its broken pincer like a club to beat Grey Cloak. He leaped over the claw, did a somersault in midair, and landed perfectly on the crab's back. Using both hands, he plunged his burning steel into the crab's brain. The shell cracked, and mystic fire burst through its limbs. Its efforts to drag Dyphestive into the chilling depths stopped.

Dyphestive sat up and started prying open the pincer locked on his leg. "Sweet Gapoli, it's like a vise!"

Nearby, the crabs crawled out of the water and scurried onto the beach.

Grey Cloak started hacking at the bottom of the dead crab's pincer. "Dirty acorns, these things are tough!"

"You don't have to tell me!" Dyphestive latched his fingers on the lower pincer and heaved. "Urk!"

"Put some muscle into it, brother!" Grey Cloak said as he saw mounds of muscle and veins pop out on his brother's arms, neck, and temples.

The crab pincer cracked and split away from the husk of the main claw. Dyphestive pulled his leg free and crab-walked up the bank and away from their pursuers.

Grey Cloak helped his brother to the top of the bank. "Can you walk?"

Dyphestive stared down at his bloody ankle. "As long as I have both feet, I can walk."

The other giant crabs didn't show any interest in pursuit and slunk back into the water.

Grey Cloak shook his head. "Spiders and crabs and zombies, oh my."

"What is going on down there?" Gorva shouted. "What are you standing around for?"

"We're going! We're going!" Grey Cloak noticed another tunnel like the one they'd entered from on the other side and said, "That must be where the spiders took Jakoby."

"After you," Dyphestive said.

"Here, you're going to need this." He handed Dyphestive his long sword. "You really need to take better care of your equipment."

"Don't remind me. I found myself attached to the iron

sword. I'm going to miss it." Dyphestive spun the long sword on his wrist. "It's small, but thanks."

"Small. Ha, you're too big." Grey Cloak led the way into the tunnel, which had the same dimensions as the last one. Torches were bracketed to the wall, and at the tunnel's end was a flickering burning light like one would see in a fireplace. "Well, it's clear that men made these tunnels at some point in time, but who?"

"Perhaps Thannis collapsed on another subterranean city," Dyphestive suggested.

"That would mean that something else lived down here before, and aside from spiders and crabs, I see no other evidence of that."

The end of the tunnel opened into a circular-domed chamber that was perfectly built from the rock. Strands of webbing and spiderwebs decorated the better part of the room. Giant ruby-like stones in the outer wall glowed with their own fire. A golden glint immediately caught Grey Cloak's eye, and he looked down at the floor. He tapped his brother's shoulder and said, "Look down."

Dyphestive dropped his stare.

The chamber floor was covered in treasure from one end to the other. Among the tremendous piles of ancient coins were precious stones, gold and silver chalices, plates and flatware, weapons, armor, and the bones of many skeletons.

"This sort of place would make Batram drool," Grey

Cloak said as he wiped his mouth. "It's making *me* drool." He bent over and reached for a small golden jewelry box lying near his toes.

Dyphestive grabbed him, pulled him up, and said, "I wouldn't do that if I were you."

Grey Cloak narrowed his eyes.

Spiders nested in the webs extended their legs, which they had balled up into their bodies. They began to crawl and climb over the webbing.

"I think I'm getting sick of spiders," Grey Cloak said.

"*You're* getting sick? How do you think I feel?" Jakoby said. He was in the back of the room, covered in webbing and fastened to a throne-like golden chair. Two spiders were latched on top of him, their fangs fastened to his limbs. "In the name of the Monarchy, get these things off me!"

37

DYPHESTIVE AND GREY CLOAK raced across the treasure chamber, kicking up coins in their wake.

Grey Cloak arrived at Jakoby's chair first, slid across the treasure, and stabbed a spider in the side with his dagger. The spider detached from Jakoby and scurried away. Dyphestive skewered the second spider, lifted it off with his sword, and flung it away.

The spiders burst into activity. They crawled down the walls and shot down the webbing.

"Get this off me!" Jakoby demanded.

"There's no time!" Grey Cloak said.

The spiders closed in from all directions.

"Dyphestive, catch!" He tossed his dagger to his brother, who snatched it out of the air.

"What are you going to fight with?" Dyphestive asked.

Grey Cloak knelt and filled his hands full of ancient coins. He fed his power into the metal and knit his brow. "Watch and see!" He slung a handful of glowing coins into the oncoming wave of spiders. The metal cut into them and blew away their limbs.

"I like it!" Dyphestive's arms started pumping steel deep into the spiders' bodies. *Glitch! Gurk! Slice! Gorch!*

"That's it, Dyphestive!" Jakoby roared. "Stomp the spider goo out of them!"

Grey Cloak moved like the wind, slinging coins and blowing spiders to pieces.

What Dyphestive didn't stab, he stomped the life out of with his boots. A spider dropped on his back and sank its teeth into the back of his neck. He turned his back to his brother and said, "Grey, hit me!"

Grey Cloak flicked a coin and blew a hole in the spider. It sprayed goo and dropped dead on the floor.

Another wave of spiders raced toward them. They were fast, but Grey Cloak proved faster. He scooped up handfuls of more coins and wrought havoc. "You've tasted my thunder. Now feel the burn!"

Boom! Boom! Boom! Boom!

The quicker, stronger, and more powerful Grey Cloak and Dyphestive outmatched the small horde of spiders and mutilated every last one of them.

Dyphestive's sword and dagger hung at his sides. He was up to his elbows in spider gore.

Grey Cloak wiped bug splatter from his face and said, "That was easy." He retrieved his dagger from his brother and used it to cut away Jakoby's silky bonds. "Are you well?"

Jakoby rubbed the bite marks on his forearms. "My head is light from the blood they sucked out of me, but I'll live." He dropped a heavy hand on Grey Cloak's shoulder. "Thank you both. The truth is that I didn't think I would make it, like Dalsay said."

"Well, what does he know?" Grey Cloak sheathed his dagger and began to mosey through the treasure chamber. "Look at all of this. Fantastic!"

"More than we can carry—that is for certain." Dyphestive kicked a dead spider out of the way and began to wander around the room. "Have you ever seen so much treasure, Jakoby?"

"Monarch City has several vaults such as this that I guarded when I was younger. It wouldn't surprise me a bit if this was one of many," he responded.

"Several?" Dyphestive asked.

Jakoby nodded. He made his way over to a suit of plate armor that lay on the ground and knelt. A skeleton was still inside it. "Lords of Thunder, this man wears the seal of a Monarch Knight. I had a suit the same as this once. He must have been part of the expeditions. It seems we've made it as far as they did, but they didn't make it out of here."

"No, but we will. After all, we've made it this far." Grey

Cloak stood beside a stone table with treasure piled on top. There were tiaras, crowns, bracelets, and necklaces lying among the coins. He picked up a jewel-encrusted crown and set it cockeyed on his head. "How do I look? Could I pass for a Monarch?"

"Only if you come from Monarch blood or marry into it," Jakoby said. "Or you can buy your way in if you have enough. This vault would be enough."

"I like that idea."

"But why would you want to be a Monarch? They are a very detached society. Believe me, I've seen it."

Grey Cloak dropped the crown back onto the table. "We have more important matters to worry about than being rich, I suppose. We still have to save Gorva and destroy the lich and her army of zombies." Cold metal coins slid underneath his steps. "It's best we take it one evil minion at a time."

Jakoby unfastened a sword belt from the corpse and buckled it around his waist. "Impressive. There is corrosion on the metal, but the leather's still pliable. I wonder what took this man. His weapons weren't drawn. There is no major scarring on the armor." He drew the sword. It came out of the sheath with a ring of metal. The blade shone like daylight, and with wide eyes, he said, "Lords of the Monarch, what a sword!"

"I wouldn't get attached. According to Mortis, we won't be able to keep any of this," Grey Cloak said. "But we might be able to use it." He picked up a coin from another table. Everything in the piles was covered in a fine green grit. He rubbed it off on his fingers. "It must be the dampness."

"What was that?" Jakoby sheathed his sword then drew it again in the wink of an eye. "Beautiful."

"I was curious about all the grit, but why should I expect anything different in a damp spider lair?"

"Uh, Grey, you might want to come and take a look at this," Dyphestive said from the other side of the room.

He picked his way across the room, avoiding the dead spiders and the skeletons that had been picked clean by the spiders, he assumed. "Yes, what is it?"

Dyphestive pointed at a standing suit of armor propped up in the corner.

Grey Cloak gasped.

38

"I CAN'T BELIEVE MY EYES," Grey Cloak whispered. "Can it be?"

Draped over the standing suit of armor's shoulders was a broken-in grey cloak.

He eased his fingers toward the fabric. "It must be a trick." Two fingers brushed over the soft fabric, which felt unlike anything he'd ever felt before. He glanced at his brother. "This is it."

"The Cloak of Legends?"

"I'd know it anywhere," he replied.

Jakoby cleared his throat, caught their attention, and said, "There is something oddly familiar about these dead bodies on the floor." He poked at the air. "But I can't put my finger on it. This sword belt, for example, fits my hips perfectly."

Grey Cloak returned his attention to the cloak and rubbed his jaw. "How could I have been here before and done this? Do you think I did this?"

Dyphestive shrugged. "Someone did. It looks intentional." He stared hard at the great sword gripped in the hands of the suit of full plate armor. The metal gauntlets' fingers were wrapped around the hilt of the sword, which was pointed toward the ground. His head leaned farther over his shoulder as he studied the crusty sword. "It looks like the iron sword," he said.

Grey Cloak tore his eyes away from the cloak and looked at the blade. "It does look the same as the iron sword. The handguard and pommel are the same, but look at that." A square gem was built into the sword's cross guard on the right, below the blade. He scratched the grit away with his finger. The gemstone twinkled with bloodred fire. "I think it's magic, maybe."

Jakoby tapped them both on the shoulders and said, "I thought the spiders made my skin crawl, but I think I found something worse. Come." He led them through the chamber, taking note of the bodies he came across. "This one is a knight like me." He moved away. "Not much left of this one, but look at the teeth. Orcen. Over here is a man, I believe. Look at his leather armor and all the blades he once carried." He pointed. "And there." He hurried over to a set of bones and knelt then lifted a sash wrapped around a very small waist. "Leena wears robes such as these. Don't you agree?"

Dyphestive's face paled.

"It has to be a coincidence. It can't be her." Grey Cloak's eyes swept through the room. Jakoby's theory had accounted for every person in their party except for Dyphestive, Grey Cloak, and one other. A smallish skeleton woman in familiar clothing lay against a table. "Zora!"

The skeleton wore a pair of tall boots, and a black scarf was tied around her neck. "This is impossible. It can't be them. It must be some sort of a trick. An illusion. It must be the doing of Mortis."

Dyphestive sat on both knees, holding what could have been Leena's long ponytail. "It feels real, but where are we, brother?"

"I don't know." Grey Cloak marched over to the suit of armor, gathered his cloak, and put it on. A familiar warmth spread through his extremities. "We need to move." He started peeling the gauntlet's fingers away from the iron sword. A black staff, four feet long, fell from behind the blade. He caught it in his right hand. "What's this?"

"A cane?" Dyphestive asked.

"It's too long to be a cane. It's more of a walking stick. But why would I put it here?" He spun it around in his hand. "It looks more like something your woman would carry." He eyed the dead body that they thought could be

Leena. "Not that one, naturally. But who could be absolutely certain, seeing how neither one of them speaks?"

"Grey Cloak," Dyphestive said with a growl in his voice, "that's not nice."

"No, I don't suppose it is," he said, running his gaze along the staff. He noticed runes and symbols carved along the length of the polished wood. "It must be here for some reason. Nevertheless, we need to get out of here."

"What about the figurine?" Dyphestive asked.

Grey Cloak gave a nervous laugh. "Forgive my excitement. My reunion with my cloak got the best of me, but I didn't see it anywhere in this chamber."

"No offense, but we haven't been looking that long," Dyphestive said. "We need to keep looking."

"Agreed," he replied.

"I'm not going to spend the rest of my life down here like the rest of them," Jakoby said. "My bones are itching. We need to hurry."

As Grey Cloak waded through the treasure trove, a thought came to mind. *No, it couldn't be that easy. Could it?*

He started patting himself down and reached into the inner pockets of the cloak. A familiar object filled his hand. He pulled out a black figurine of a faceless man. It was as smooth as polished onyx or black jade. His smile could have filled the room. He cleared his throat and caught the others' attention. "Look what I found."

Dyphestive stared at him with disbelief. "You found it? Where was it?"

"In my cloak pocket."

"Are you certain that's it?" Jakoby asked.

Grey Cloak polished the figurine on the sleeve of his robes. "Oh, this is it. I can tell by the surface and the heft. There is nothing like it in all the world." He recalled the word of power.

Osid-ayan-umra-shokrah-ha!

The figurine stayed cool to the touch.

Will it work, or will it not? That is the question.

He hid the figurine back in his cloak. "Grab anything that might be useful. We're still going to have to fight our way out of here." He found some potion vials, a scroll, and some other trinkets and fed them into his pockets. He hugged himself. "I'm so glad to have my cloak back."

Water began to spill into the chamber from the mouth of the tunnel and rose like a creek. It covered their feet in seconds.

"The chamber is flooding!" Jakoby hollered. "We need to go now!" He headed up the steps that led out of the chamber. A tide waist high knocked him backward. "Monarchs!"

"Grey Cloak," Dyphestive said. He wore a huge gold necklace with a cross on it. "I don't think we're going to be allowed to leave here with the treasure."

"And this explains what happened to the others—they

drowned," Jakoby added. The water flooded in so fast that it was up to their knees. "We're doomed!"

"No, we aren't!" Grey Cloak knew the cloak would allow him to swim underwater, but that wouldn't save the others. He waded toward the tunnel.

A tremendous figure dropped from the shadows in the ceiling and blocked his path.

"Zooks!"

39

THE MONSTER BLOCKING the tunnel was twice their size. It stood on two powerful legs and had a head like a bat and four pairs of eyes. Sets of feathery gills flexed on its neck. Its body was covered in fishlike scales, and it had four muscular humanoid arms and four spider legs in between.

"What sort of abomination is that?" Jakoby asked.

"I don't know, but we have to get past it!" Grey Cloak said. Without thinking, he summoned his wizard fire. The end of the four-foot staff he carried blossomed into the tip of a fiery spear. "Whoa! That will do."

The monster opened its slavering jaws. Drool spilled over its sharp fangs and down its chin. It flexed its arms and webbed hands and let out an ear-splitting roar.

Grey Cloak pinched his nose. His eyes watered. "If we can survive that smell, we can survive anything."

Dyphestive raised the iron sword. The gem in the cross guard glowed like a red-hot coal. "It's thunder time!" He stormed the monster.

Grey Cloak and Jakoby flanked Dyphestive and ascended the watery steps.

The monster made a rattling sound with its mouth. It pointed its spider legs at Dyphestive and shot long quills out. The quills stuck into Dyphestive's flesh as if he were a cushion, but it didn't slow his advance.

Grey Cloak jabbed his spear at the monster and asked, "Dyphestive, are you well?"

"We'll see!" He chopped at the monster's leg and tore through its thigh. It bled green.

"Rawr!" The monster punched Dyphestive with two of its fists and knocked him back, making him splash into the water.

Jakoby knifed his way up the stairs and stabbed the creature between the ribs. It twisted at the hip and back-handed him, knocking him into the wall.

"Get back!" Grey Cloak poked at the creature's webbed hands, keeping the sharp talons of its fingers at bay. "Back!"

"Grey Cloak, you must shut off the water! You need to hurry!" Dalsay said. He appeared in front of the monster, whose claws passed right through him.

"Oh, now you show up!" Grey Cloak ducked under the monster's outstretched hands. "What am I supposed to do?"

"The river has been dammed. You need to open it. Follow me, and I'll show you what to do," Dalsay replied as he waved him toward the tunnel.

"Easier said than done, wizard! In case you hadn't noticed, there is a small obstacle in the way!"

"I'm sure you'll think of something." Dalsay vanished down the tunnel.

Dyphestive rose from the water with a determined look on his face. Knees pumping, he went after the monster. "Grey Cloak, we'll distract it. You go!"

"I'm not leaving you behind!"

"Go, Grey Cloak!" Jakoby shouted from the other side of the steps. "Your brother and I will handle this monstrosity!"

They rushed the monster and thrust their steel into its flesh. It belted out a roar.

Grey Cloak snuck behind the monster and dove into the rising water. The tunnel had filled above his shoulders, and the water pushed him back toward the chamber. He dipped his head under. *Here we go, cloak. Do your thing!*

The Cloak of Legends took over the same as it had in Lake Flugen. It propelled him under the surface, and he swam like a fish.

He popped up on the other side of the tunnel and treaded water. Dalsay hovered over the surface with his arms crossed over his chest. The river water had risen over the bridge.

"Well?" Grey Cloak asked.

"This way!" Dalsay led him downriver to where the water flowed through the rock. "The opening is dammed. I watched as a trap door fell and sealed it shut."

"What am I supposed to do about it?"

"There has to be a release that will lift the seal back up. Find it! And hurry, or everyone will drown."

"Yes, I'd figured that much out." He sank into the water and saw the huge stone seal that blocked the tunnel. It was surrounded by giant crabs.

40

"MY SWORD IS SHARP, but this monster feels no pain!" Jakoby said. He ducked under the claws of a webbed hand and stabbed the monster in the stomach. "Die! Curse you!"

Dyphestive fared little better. He chopped off two spider arms and gored the monster in the chest, but it still kept coming. "I feel your pain!" He pushed out of the chest-high water and executed an awkward overhead chop. The blade sliced through the monster's forearm and bit through the bone of its shoulder.

The monster brought two fists down like clubs and slammed them into Dyphestive's shoulders. The jarring blow drove him under the water. *Bloody Biscuits!*

The fight went on, back and forth. The monster struck, then Dyphestive and Jakoby let steel cut into its abdomen and limbs. All the while, the water continued to rise, making it impossible for them to keep their footing.

"Keep swinging! It has to die eventually!" Dyphestive hollered and gave a sword thrust that pierced bone.

Jakoby spit out a mouthful of water and replied, "Not if we drown first."

The monster ducked beneath the water and vanished.

"Where did it go?" Jakoby asked. His head was bleeding, and he gasped. "And I'm standing on my tiptoes! Are you?!"

Eyeing the water, Dyphestive nodded. He was a little taller than Jakoby, but it wouldn't be long before they were both completely submerged. "I think we hurt it. Now it's waiting for us to drown to finish us."

"That's what I'd do," Jakoby said. "We aren't going to float carrying this steel either. We need to kill it and—*ulp!*"

Jakoby was jerked under the surface. His arms waved above the water then vanished.

"Horseshoes!" Dyphestive took a deep breath, dropped his sword, and dove into the water. Two bodies thrashed. He swam like a frog toward the melee. The monster had Jakoby in a stranglehold. Jakoby whacked at its side with his sword.

Dyphestive swam underneath the monster's legs and snuck behind it. He bunched his legs under him and launched. With a mighty effort, he climbed onto the monster's back and put it in a headlock and squeezed.

The monster thrashed from side to side. Its shoulders and hips twisted violently, and it stormed through the water.

With one arm around its bull neck and the other hand locked to his wrist, he yanked back. The muscles in his arms knotted up, and he squeezed the bat head and crushed it like a vise.

His lungs started to burn, but so did the fire within. *Die, monster! Die!*

He spit out air bubbles and let out his own watery yell.

The monster's strong limbs trembled. It spasmed and jerked. The hard muscles in its neck caved against the pressure. Its spine snapped. *Pop!*

Dyphestive paddled to the surface and, gasping, came face-to-face with Jakoby. "Are you—*eeyah!*"

The monster floated up between them. It was on its back, and its neck was bent, a dagger stuck in it.

Using the monster for a raft, Jakoby pulled the dagger free. "We did it," he said, panting. "I don't know how, but we did."

Dyphestive nodded.

The water continued to rise, and they floated ever closer to the ceiling.

"We need to swim out of here," Jakoby said.

"There's nowhere to go," Dyphestive said. "If it's flooded on this side, it will be flooded on the other side too. It's in Grey Cloak's hands now."

Grey Cloak thrust his spear into a giant crab, searing it inside and out. It floated down into the watery depths, and three others came forward.

Great! At least I can swim like a fish!

The Cloak of Legends's unique powers lent him the ability to breathe, see, and swim fast underwater. Using his superior maneuverability, he weaved through the slowly swimming crabs and gored them individually.

Finally!

Using his spear for light, he searched the seal in the tunnel. It was made of tons of rock and was impossible for him to move.

What did Dalsay say? Look for a trigger or a release.

Grey Cloak ran his hands along every nook and cranny near the seal. He didn't see a lever or handle of any sort. He swam back to the surface and shouted, "Dalsay! I don't see anything! Do you?"

"I'm looking!"

"Someone must have set it off. Did you see anyone?"

"No one is here but us," Dalsay replied.

"And me!" Gorva yelled. "Find it or we are going to drown!"

The chamber was three-quarters filled.

Grey Cloak spun around as he treaded water, searching the ceiling. He tried to understand the trap. *The purpose is to flood the chamber. Once the chamber is flooded, the trap needs to be set again, and it needs to be drained. No one could swim down here. Hence, it must be triggered by something.*

Half-hidden in the webbing, mounted in the ceiling, was a bronze plate with three wavy lines.

"Aha!" he said.

"What?" Gorva asked.

He swam underneath the plate. "I bet my pointed ears that's a pressure plate. Except I can't reach it. Hold on." He dove deep in the water, turned, and swam upward, gaining speed, then burst out of the water like a fish. He hit the bronze plate with his staff and pushed. The pressure plate clicked.

Grey Cloak clung to the ceiling, using the webbing to hold him fast.

Below the water's surface, stone ground against stone. The water bubbled and started to churn. A whirlpool formed beneath them.

"Will you free me?" Gorva demanded.

"Do you want me to free you now? You'll drop into that whirlpool."

"As soon as it's finished, you get me out of these webs," she said.

"I will." He glanced about. "Where are the spiders?"

"They aren't foolish," she said. "They scurried out of the tunnel the moment the water started to rise."

41

THE UNDERWATER RIVER DRAINED, and Grey Cloak found two soaking-wet men back inside the flooded tunnel chamber. He gave Dyphestive a bear hug, even though he had a hard time wrapping his arms around him. "Brother, you are well! I'm elated!"

Dyphestive thumped him on the back and said, "Thanks to your efforts. It came down to the final moments, though."

Jakoby poured the water out of one of his boots and said, "You have my thanks as well. I've envisioned myself perishing by the sword many times but never water. A watery death would have been far worse."

The deeper section of the treasure chamber was still flooded. The coins and gems shone beneath the calm water, and the monster floated on top.

Gorva stormed down the tunnel with Dalsay in tow. Her gaze passed over the men and set on the floating monster. Her lips twisted, and she asked, "What is that thing?"

"We were hoping you would know," Dyphestive said.

She gave him a serious look. "Why would you think I would know?"

The men chuckled.

Gorva waded deeper into the room and said, "Your humor is sad. Great dragons!" She rushed into the water below the tunnel then dove in and came up with her arms full of dripping treasure. "Look at this hoard!"

"That's the reason we almost died," Grey Cloak said. "We can't take it with us."

"We can take some." Her big eyes reflected the gold she held. "It would be a waste not to."

Dalsay stood at the tunnel's entrance and said, "We have more important matters to worry about than treasure. We have a lich and her zombie army that need to be dealt with. Find a weapon to fight with. You're going to need it."

"That won't be a problem." Gorva waded through the water.

Grey Cloak caught Dalsay studying his staff. "What?"

"Those are some interesting items that you have acquired," Dalsay said. "Did you find the figurine?"

Grey Cloak hadn't even had time to think about it. He

considered not telling Dalsay but opted for the truth. "I have it."

Dalsay nodded.

"Did you know all these items were here all along?" he asked.

"I only knew of the figurine. And nothing has changed. We still don't have a prayer to escape Thannis—at least *you* don't—but you made it this far. There is a sliver of hope." He approached Grey Cloak, and a whimsical smile crossed his face. "Life never ceases to amaze me."

Grey Cloak twirled the staff under his arm. "What do you mean by that?"

"There isn't enough time to explain. But that staff you carry, I've seen it before, long ago. It's called the Wand of Weapons."

"Where did you see it?"

"As I said, we don't have time."

Gorva emerged dripping wet from the water. She carried a spear and had a sword belt crossed over her back. "I'm ready to get out of this spider-infested sewer." She walked right through Dalsay. "I'm not waiting anymore."

They hurried through the exit tunnel, crossed the bridge, and made their return trip to the heart of Thannis. Everyone's boots squished with every step, except for Grey Cloak, who was barefoot.

Water dripped from the ceiling, and the flood water

continued to drain. Their footsteps splashed over the slick surface. No spiders appeared. Nothing slowed their trek.

Grey Cloak sped ahead as they neared the well they'd entered. He thought of Zora.

I hope she's there.

The top of the huge well loomed above like a skylight. He jumped over the rocks and hurried up the spiral stairs. The once-empty streets were busy again with the wandering dead. The pavement surrounding the well opening was covered in water. There were no signs of Zora or Leena.

Zooks!

He climbed out of the well. The undead paid him no mind and went about their business. He scanned the area as the others climbed out.

"Where's Zora?" Dyphestive asked.

"I don't know. I'm looking," he said without hiding his irritation.

"Judging by the new activity, I believe our enemies think that we're dead," Dalsay said. "This could be a good thing."

"Nothing could be good if Zora is missing." Grey Cloak felt a tap on his shoulder. "What, Dyphestive?"

"Huh?" his brother asked from the other side of the well.

The scent of jasmine caught Grey Cloak's nose, then

Zora appeared and threw her arms around him. "You're alive! Thank goodness you are alive!"

"Thank goodness *you* are alive," he said. "Are you well? What happened?"

"Where's Leena?" Dyphestive asked with concern.

Zora pointed at the entrance to an old tavern. Leena sat on the end of the porch with her legs kicking.

Dyphestive smiled and hurried over to her.

"I thought you were dead, but we waited," Zora said. "What happened down there?"

"What happened up *here*?"

Zora broke off her embrace and said, "I'll tell you what happened. My heart almost burst. We heard a roar of water inside the well. Without warning, more spiders scurried out. I thought I'd die. But they didn't attack. They came and kept going. Shortly after that, water bubbled over the rim of the well, soaking the streets." She clasped his hand and kissed it. "I thought for certain you were all gone. Still, we waited. Shortly after the flood, the undead returned to the streets. The same as before, they looked right through us."

He turned his attention to Dalsay. "If they think we're dead, we can slip out of here, can't we?"

"That's unlikely."

"Why?"

Dalsay's wide sleeve hung low from his bony arm as he pointed. Thannis's zombie soldiers marched down the street, making a beeline for the company.

"They know we're here," Dalsay said.

"What do we do?" Zora asked.

"There's only one way out of Thannis alive," Dalsay said. "We must kill Mortis."

The slow march of the zombie soldiers turned into a run.

"To the temple!" Dalsay ordered. "Everyone, run!"

42

RAZOR

"LITTLE? WHO ARE YOU CALLING LITTLE?" Razor watched the man called Ghost dismount. He wore a worn leather mask dyed blue and moved over the ground without a sound. "And what is the situation with the masks? Are all of you as ugly as you sound?"

Ghost reached over his shoulder and drew his long sword from his scabbard. The blade snaked out of its sheath without a sound.

"One sword, eh? Against my two? You might want to reconsider, fella," Razor warned. He stole a glance at Scar and Shamrok, who let out rusty chuckles. Their voices made his skin crawl. "You fellas have quite a sense of humor, seeing how your friend is about to die."

"He's not the one that's going to die." Shamrok leaned

back in his saddle and crossed his arms over his chest. "I'll bet my life on that."

Razor fixed his attention on Ghost. Unlike the other men, his eyes were black pits. "At least you don't flap your lips like the others."

Ghost stormed forward and swung. Metal kissed metal in a ring of steel. Razor caught his attacker's blade between both of his. The jarring impact rattled his arms to the elbows.

Bloody biscuits, he's strong! But is he fast?

He spun away from Ghost and unleashed a backhand swing at the Doom Rider's thigh. Ghost blocked the strike and countered with a stab at Razor's throat.

Razor snaked his head aside and brought both of his swords up to bear. Ghost hammered away at him with both hands on the handle of his sword. Razor shuffled backward.

He's fast!

Clang!

And strong!

Bang!

He parried for his life.

He's not a man. He's a force!

Razor had faced the finest swordsmen in the land and never met his match, but they weren't men like that one.

Ghost's sword snaked through his defense and clipped him across his cheek.

"First blood!" Scar hollered. "That didn't take long!"

"Let him catch his breath, Ghost!" Shamrok said. "Don't end it quickly. We haven't had this much fun in days."

Warm blood ran over Razor's cheek.

Hold it together!

He paced back and forth, eyeing his enemy.

I can beat him. This is the fight I've been waiting for.

"Uh-oh, it looks like someone is getting mad. You'd better be careful, Ghost. He might bleed tears all over you," Scar said.

"The only one that is going to bleed is you, Red Face." Razor spit and squared off on Ghost.

I know how fast he is. I know how strong he is. I know how skilled he is.

He grinned.

But I haven't shown him how good I am.

He beckoned Ghost over with his short sword. "Let's keep dancing."

Scar guffawed. "Look at the bow in this young man's back. I like it."

Ghost set his shoulders and came right at Razor.

Razor went on the offense and met the Doom Rider with spinning steel. His arms pumped out lightning-quick strokes. Ghost stood his ground, parried, shifted from side to side, and shuffled his feet. The damp air filled with the chorus of the ring of steel.

The Doom Rider fought off every attack, so Razor turned up the heat. *Clang! Bang! Chop! Hack! Slice! Stab!*

He snuck that last strike between Ghost's defenses and buried his short sword deep in the Doom Rider's chest. "You didn't see that coming, did you?" He shoved the blade clean through.

Ghost let out a raspy sigh of cold fetid breath.

"Ooh," Razor said, "what was your last meal? Rotten fish?" He pushed the man away and slid his sword free. His gaze switched between Scar and Shamrok. He could see the whites of their eyes hidden in their masks. "Which one of you sack faces is next?"

They sat on their gourns and didn't say a word.

"That's what I thought." He sheathed his blades and swung his gaze toward Drysis. "We're finished here. It's best that you be on your way," he said.

Drysis returned a cold gaze, leaned forward, and said, "You are mistaken, Razor. Your fight isn't over." Her gaze passed over his shoulder.

He turned and found Ghost standing and looking right at him. "Impossible. You're dead."

Ghost's arms shot out, and he locked his fingers around Razor's throat then lifted him off the ground by the neck.

"There's a reason we call him Ghost, you fool!" Scar said. "He's already dead."

Razor's eyes bulged in their sockets. He chopped at

Ghost's rigid arms with his fists. Ghost walked him across the ground.

He dropped his hands to his sides and took two daggers from his hips. He jammed them into Ghost's ribs. Ghost only squeezed harder.

Die, blast you!

He kicked and kneed the undead man. In the background, he could hear Scar and Shamrok laughing.

"Don't kill him, Ghost. I don't want him dead. I want him broken," Drysis ordered.

Ghost slammed Razor hard into the ground then pinned him by the neck and started punching him in the ribs.

"Hit him for us, Ghost!" Shamrok said. "Hit him hard!"

43

GHOST BEAT RAZOR LIKE A DRUM. His ribs cracked, and he began to wheeze.

Razor jammed every small blade he had into the Doom Rider's body, but the blows kept coming.

"Enough!" Drysis said.

The Doom Rider stood over Razor. Daggers were stuck in his ribs, leg, and abdomen, but he didn't bleed.

Razor spit out a tooth and asked, "What's the matter? Are you getting tired?"

"He might not fight well, but at least he has spirit," Scar said with a nod. "Respect."

"You know where you can stick your respect." Razor rolled over to his hands and knees. Pain lanced through his body. His lungs burned. He tried to stand.

Ghost stepped on his back and pushed him down.

He let out a painful gasp and said, "Fighting with your feet, eh? That's low, even for a worm-eater like you." With one arm extended and the other hidden under his gut, he got ahold of his short sword's grip. "Where are we going with this? What do you want to know?"

"Ah, we have cooperation. I like the sound of promise," Drysis the Dreadful responded. "Tell us who you're traveling with."

"Yuh, Lone Blade, spit it out!" Shamrok said.

Ghost removed his foot from Razor's back.

One way or the other, they're going to kill me. But I'll keep it interesting. To the end.

He tightened his grip on his sword, started to rise, and slumped down again. *Need to sell it.* He let out a painful gasp.

"That sounds bad," Scar said. "I bet he has a cracked rib or two."

"I'd say four or five. I'm pretty sure I heard them snap," Shamrok commented.

"Why don't you come over here and count for yourselves!" Razor sucked air through his teeth. "Lords of Steel!" He fought his way up to his knees but kept his head down and slumped over.

"We're waiting," Drysis said.

"Give a fella a moment to catch his breath, will you?" He closed his eyes and took a deep breath through his nose. He envisioned Ghost's position and exactly where he was going to strike. He tilted his head back, took a breath, and said, "Now, what was the question?"

Drysis groaned. "You're wasting time. Who do you travel with?"

Razor pulled his sword and twisted at the hips. He put all of his strength and momentum into the swing. The blade whistled through the air. *Slice!*

Flashing steel bit clean through Ghost's knee and severed it from the leg. Ghost wobbled.

In the same moment, Razor rose and hacked Ghost's sword arm off at the elbow. Limb and steel fell flat on the ground.

Razor was in the zone. He moved with alarming speed without thinking. He zeroed in on Ghost's neck. His short sword rose and started down. *Clatch-Zip!*

A javelin of fire ripped through his right shoulder and spun him around. He faced Drysis with a bolt in his shoulder, and his sword fell from his fingers. She pumped the handle of her crossbow, instantly loading another bolt, and squeezed the trigger. *Clatch-Zip!*

A second bolt whizzed into his belly.

"Augh!" Razor stumbled backward, tripped over a boulder, and fell onto his back. He rolled back up to his side and stood again.

Scar and Shamrok jumped from their gourns and came at him with swords.

Razor drew his last long sword from his back with his

good arm. He licked his lips and said, "Here come the cowards. Prepare to die, worms!" He lunged at Scar.

Scar swept the blade aside with a block so hard that it knocked the blade free from Razor's fingers.

He stumbled, clutching his burning gut, and fell. When he looked up, Scar and Shamrok loomed over him with their blades at his neck. "If I didn't have two holes in me, the both of you'd be dead by now." He managed a painful laugh. "Look at your friend over there. His arm and leg are missing."

Scar poised his blade to strike. "We'll have the final word."

"Scar, no!" Drysis said as she dismounted. "I need him alive."

"Heh, heh, heh, a good thing your mother is protecting you, or you'd both be in worse shape than your two-limbed friend," he said.

Scar kicked him in the gut, and Shamrok did the same. Razor groaned loudly.

"Pick him up," Drysis ordered.

The Doom Riders lifted him off the ground and held him before Drysis.

Razor caught his first good look at Drysis the Dreadful. She had an eye as black as coal and pale, almost white skin with blue veins showing. "I bet you were a pretty sight once, but you're nothing but ugly now."

She clamped her hand over his jaw and said, "You are

very chatty."

"It's part of my charm."

With her free hand, she twisted the bolt in his shoulder. "Gaaah!"

"Let us rip the information out of him, Drysis," Scar said. "It would be our pleasure."

"Don't be a fool. This man will die before he betrays his friends." Slowly, she started pulling the bolt in his shoulder free. "He is rich in character. A rare quality I despise. Fortunately, I have means to pry the information that I need out of him before he dies."

"I'm not going anywhere," Razor said.

"Your gut wound is grave." She tossed the bolt aside. "You won't survive but will experience a slow and agonizing death." She flipped the eye patch over her left eye up.

Razor tilted his head to one side. A bright-blue sapphire burned inside her eye socket and locked on him. "How much is that thing worth?" An unseen force invaded the deepest recesses of his mind. His past flashed before his eyes. His strongest memories were being dredged up to the surface, from his earliest childhood and beyond. His entire life was exposed. "No, no, stop it. Stop it, please!"

"Tell me what I want to know," Drysis suggested. "Tell me who you travel with."

Razor's iron will bent like a spoon. The walls of his mind collapsed. In a dreamlike state, he said, "I'll tell you everything you want to know."

44

THE RUINS OF THANNIS

GREY CLOAK LED Talon down the street with the zombie army on their tail. He waved his arm behind him. "This way! This way!" He turned the corner of the next block and came face-to-face with another zombie army. He skidded to a stop. "That way! That way!"

The company took off at a dead sprint down an alley.

"There's too many of them!" Gorva shouted.

"At least they aren't spiders," Zora added.

Grey Cloak didn't comment. Instead, he picked his way through the alleys, hoping to mislead the zombies and lose them.

"Grey Cloak, where are you taking us?" Zora asked. "We're going in circles."

"I know what I'm doing." He jetted down a narrow alley

and raced by another one that was logjammed with zombies. "Don't go that way."

They moved deeper into the bowels of the city. The streets buzzed with the noise of zombie soldiers on the loose. He stopped at an alley exit that led into one of the main streets. Zombie citizens wandered the city in an ordinary fashion, going about their daily business. He heard his comrades panting and looked back at the sweat glistening on their faces.

"I think we have an opening," he said.

"Where did the wizard go?" Gorva asked.

"He doesn't share the same worries we have." Grey Cloak looked down the street both ways, and two blocks down, the zombie soldiers ran with their backs to them. "We're clear. Come on and keep it slow."

"Slow? Why?" Zora asked.

"I don't want to draw the other zombies' attention, since it looks like only the soldiers are after us. And keep it quiet." He ambled into the street at a slow walk with his neck bent and put a hitch in his step.

"This looks ridiculous," Zora said.

Everyone followed suit, except for Gorva, who walked tall and with her head held high.

"Gorva!" he whispered. "To get along, you have to play along."

"I'm not doing that. Zombies are stupid. They don't

know what we're doing," Gorva said. "I'm tired of running. I want to kill them."

"You can't kill them if they're dead," he said.

Gorva snorted.

They were halfway across the street when a small group of zombie children wandered into their midst. The children were playing with steel barrel rings, rolling them down the street. Several of the children bumped right into them and fell down, letting out high-pitched screams.

The awful sound caught the other zombies' attention, and they started wandering the company's way. Farther down the street, the zombie army halted its chase and turned.

A zombie child latched onto Gorva's leg and sank his teeth into her thigh.

"Ow! Get this thing off me!"

All of a sudden, zombies burst out of the nearby buildings' doors and windows. They were a mix of men, women, soldiers, and children.

Dyphestive grabbed the child and flung it across the street into a barren water trough. "What are we waiting for, Grey? Go!"

The company fought their way through the undead children scratching and biting at their legs and raced down the open end of the street.

Grey Cloak rounded the next corner and saw the temple in the distance. "There!"

A blockade of zombie soldiers several men deep had set up at the base of the temple's steps.

Behind their ranks was the ghostly form of Dalsay, waving them toward the open doors. The wizard's ghostly voice carried down the street. "Hurry!"

Behind Talon, hordes of the undead closed in. Ahead, an army of zombies blocked the temple with sharp steel and gnashing teeth.

"We'll never make it through there," Gorva said. "There are too many."

Dyphestive stepped to the front with a white-knuckled grip on the handle of his sword. Fire burned in his eyes. The gemstone on his sword's cross guard gleamed like a bright bloodred star. "I'll make a hole."

Grey Cloak put a hand on Dyphestive's shoulder and said, "Brother, no. There must be another way."

"There's only one way." Dyphestive pointed his sword at the temple. His jaw muscles clenched. "That way!" He tore away from Grey Cloak's grip, and with long strides, he raced down the road. "It's thunder time!"

Leena chased Dyphestive with her nunchakus spinning.

Gorva and Jakoby moved to the fore.

"We can't let him die alone," Jakoby said. He let out a shout. "For the Monarchy!"

He and Gorva took off with their legs pumping at full speed. They left Grey Cloak and Zora in the dust.

"Stay close to me," he said to her.

"As long as there aren't any spiders, I'll be fine!" She glanced at the zombies charging down the street behind them then kissed him on the cheek, lifted the scarf over her nose, and vanished. "I'll see you in the temple."

Grey Cloak shook his head as he gazed after the others racing to their doom. "I'm going to be last. Rogues of Rodden! I'm never last, but in this case, I'll make an exception."

Dyphestive formed the tip of the wedge, with Jakoby and Gorva flanking him and Leena behind him. He smashed into the first row of zombies like a crashing wave. The iron sword swung forth in a huge sweeping arc and blasted through three zombie soldiers.

The tide of evil crashed down on the group.

Dyphestive's arms pumped with vigor. Every moving body the iron sword met fell in a streak of red. Dry bones burst. Armor rattled. Ancient bodies were stomped and crushed. A gap appeared on the steps.

"Make a hole, brother! Make a hole!" Grey Cloak shouted.

Zombie soldiers collapsed on them from all directions and buried them.

Grey Cloak couldn't see a soul in the grave of evil. He raced on with the Rod of Weapons burning bright in his hands and shouted, "Nooo!"

45

Dyphestive shoved the end of his sword through two heavily armored zombie soldiers and watched their bones collapse. A jolt of energy coursed through the sword, into his veins, and into his heaving shoulders. "Thunderbolts!" he exclaimed.

The horde of zombie soldiers crowded them from all directions. They came at them with sword and spear, but their efforts were slow and clumsy. They usually won by strength of numbers, wearing the mortal body down and finally running over them.

But that day, it was not the case. Talon battled its way up the steps, through the ranks of rotting flesh, led by the tremendous efforts of Dyphestive. The Iron Sword blasted through armor and bone. Torsos were cleaved clean through. Battered skulls exploded.

Dyphestive hollered at the top of his lungs, "Release the thunder!" He fought like a man possessed. He swung the great blade from side to side, bursting the metal shells that covered the zombies' bodies.

The undead fell in heaps. Bones were crushed underneath his boots. Three zombies fell, and five more replaced them.

Striking with precision, Gorva sliced off a zombie soldier's arm with one sword and decapitated another with her other sword. "There are too many! We need to get into the temple now!"

"It will happen!" Dyphestive said as he climbed up two more steps. They'd made it halfway up, with Dalsay waiting for them at the top. "Keep fighting!"

From behind him came a breeze on his ear and the distinctive sound of whistling. Leena fought at his back, with her glowing nunchakus spinning like wheels of fire. *Clok! Clok! Clok! Clok!*

Leena's strikes connected with deadly accuracy, striking brittle bones and turning them to dust. She drummed on a zombie's face, pulverizing its skull like an egg.

The horde kept coming.

Jakoby bellowed another battle cry. "For the Monarchy!" His sharpened steel cut off a zombie's sword arm. A backhand swing took a head from another. His long arms rose and came down with bone-jarring power. "The Monarchy!"

Talon's effort created a pocket that slowly moved up the steps. At the very top, the undead horde surged downward.

Dyphestive plowed toward the top, destroying every zombie that came into his path. "Keep going!"

Metal rang on metal. Bone popped and cracked.

They made it a quarter of the way up the steps.

"Almost there!" Dyphestive said. The door at the top was open and waiting to greet them. "Temple!"

Jakoby and Gorva's battle cries fell silent. Only the striking of metal remained.

Finally, Gorva hollered, "I can't feel my arms!"

"Keep swinging!" Jakoby said. "Keep swinging!"

Dyphestive felt their pain. His shoulders felt like anvils weighing him down. Behind him, Leena's panting was loud. "We are close!" He gored another zombie and ripped his sword out. He butchered two more where the last one fell.

Talon's strength started to fade. Their surge slowed.

Gorva screamed. "I'm wounded! My leg."

Zombies zeroed in on her blood.

Grey Cloak barred their path with the burning spear tip of his Rod of Weapons. Several quick punches of the blossoming spear point put the zombies down. "Dyphestive, make a hole to the door. Make a hole now!"

"Everybody get behind me!" Dyphestive shouted. "Here comes the thunder!" He stormed up the stone steps, plowing through a wall of zombies and running his steel through their rotten bellies.

The zombies stabbed, swung, and clawed at his arms and legs. They ripped open the flesh of his arms. But Dyphestive charged through them like a war horse. His boots found the top of the steps. A wall of zombie soldiers met him. He unleashed the iron sword and cut a corridor through them.

"Hurry! Hurry!" Dalsay shouted as he stood in the temple doorway, waving them inside. "Hurry!"

Dyphestive pushed his way into the temple. The rest of Talon stumbled in behind him.

He turned and battled the hordes of undead soldiers back. "Close the doors! Close the doors!"

Jakoby went to one door, and Grey Cloak went to the other. They shoved the long metal doors toward the threshold.

"Dyphestive, get in here!" Grey Cloak shouted. "Get in here now!"

"I'm trying!" He mowed down three more zombies. "Is everyone in?"

"Zora!" Grey Cloak called. "Zora!"

"I'm here," she said.

"We're all here!" Grey Cloak said. "Now quit playing with those zombies and get inside!"

Dyphestive backed toward the door. There was still a

crack big enough to slip through. Grey Cloak's and Jakoby's faces appeared from behind the door.

"Move your feet, man!" Jakoby said.

Dyphestive split a zombie's face open, severing it straight through the helm. "Almost finished!"

The doors slammed shut behind him with a resounding *wham*.

"What? Grey Cloak, this is no time to jest!" He stood with his back to the door and kicked it with the heel of his boot. "Let me in!" He shoved his back against it. "Let me in!"

The temple doors were sealed shut, trapping him outside with an army of zombies. They swarmed him. All he could do was swing.

46

AN UNSEEN FORCE shut the doors, as if they'd been pushed by giant invisible hands. The lock bar dropped into place, sealing Talon inside.

Grey Cloak pounded on the doors with his fists. "Nooo! Dyphestive! Dyphestive! Nooo!"

Jakoby tried to pry the bar away, shoulders heaving. "It won't budge!"

Leena whacked at the bar with her nunchakus.

"Ah-hahahaaa," came a ghostly laugh. The haunting voice echoed all over the hard walls of the temple's chamber. "Don't be so upset. Soon, your friend will join with the ranks of the undead, and you'll be with him."

Grey Cloak turned.

Mortis stood on the stage at the end of the aisle. Her rotting robes billowed around her body like a living thing.

Her pupils burned in the black depths of her eye sockets like bright stars. "I'm impressed. You survived my trap in the treasure chambers and led me to believe you were dead. But here you are, still alive. How delicious."

Grey Cloak ignited the fire on the Rod of Weapons and said, "We're going to kill you, Mortis. We're going to take that crown off your ugly head and shove it down your throat."

"A delightful idea, but how do you suppose you can kill someone that is already dead? I've had more centuries of living dead than all your group has living." Mortis walked down the steps. "You've caught my attention, however, and I offer all of you a great honor. You will be lieutenants in my army." She made a fist of bone and leathery flesh. "You will help me lead and conquer the surface together!"

"Never! You're going to pay for what you did to my friend!" Grey Cloak charged.

Mortis sent him flying backward with a flick of her wrist. His shoulder blades slammed hard into the temple door, and he collapsed onto the floor. Before he could come to his feet, Zora, Gorva, Leena, and Jakoby went flying back into the wall too. They hit the ground so hard that they were knocked out cold.

The only one left standing was Dalsay. He stood in the center aisle with Mortis walking toward him. He held out his hand and said, "Mortis, stop. I would like to parlay."

Mortis slowed her advance then came to a stop. The

towering lich looked down on Dalsay. "A parlay? Is this a jest? There is nothing that you can offer me."

"I offer flesh and blood for your bones. I offer life."

"You are a shade. You have no such power," she said.

Dalsay started speaking in an arcane tongue that Grey Cloak couldn't comprehend. The wizardly words spun and twisted on his tongue. Using the rod like a cane, he slowly started to rise with his back against the wall.

He can't stop her. He must be buying time.

Grey Cloak felt helpless. All of his friends were down. Dyphestive was trapped outside. He reached into his pocket, grabbed the Figurine of Heroes, and rubbed it. *Please work. Please work.* He uttered the word of power. "*Osid-ayan-umra-shokrah-ha!*"

No smoke spewed. Not a single spark came.

Zooks! He put the figurine away. *I guess it's up to my charm and good looks.*

"Enough chatter!" Mortis said to Dalsay. She walked through the wizard and marched toward Grey Cloak. "Your time has come to join the ranks of Thannis. Give yourself freely, and I'll make the process painless and easy."

Grey Cloak brightened. "*Painless and easy*? Ha! Why didn't you say so?" He crept closer with the rod hidden behind his back. "And you promised I'd be a lieutenant. What an honor."

Mortis tilted her head to one side, and her dry, stringy locks hung over her shoulder. She stretched out her fingers.

"You have chosen wisely, elf. Now, come closer and feed me."

As quick as a thought, Grey Cloak charged the rod with fire and rammed the spear point into Mortis's belly.

Without so much as a flinch, Mortis stood her ground and dropped her gaze on the flaming spear. "You are beginning to annoy me." She grabbed Grey Cloak by the neck of his cloak and lifted him off his feet. "The willpower of the living. I have no use for it." She tossed him over the aisle like he was made of feathers.

He made a soft landing by Dalsay.

Mortis pulled the rod free of her gut and tossed it into the pews, then she walked toward the others and set her eyes on Zora.

Grey Cloak stiffened like a board. "My limbs. What happened? I can't move."

"Her power is great," Dalsay said.

"No." He strained against his bonds with all his might. Only his lips and fingers could move. "We have to stop her, Dalsay!"

"You need to trust me."

Mortis spread out her arms. Zora's limp body rose from the floor and floated toward the glowing fingertips of the lich. Mortis cradled Zora in her arms and started to chant over her. Zora spasmed.

Grey Cloak nodded. "I trust you. I trust you. Whatever you must do, do it!"

"I'm going to join your body—entwine my spirit with yours," Dalsay said.

"You're going to what?"

Dalsay stepped into him.

Grey Cloak's eyes popped. "Whoa, I feel you. Not sure I like it."

"*You have an ability you've only begun to understand. I'm going to use it.*"

A pulse of energy burst from Grey Cloak's body and shattered the unseen force that constricted him. His arm lifted, and the Rod of Weapons flew into his hand.

Mortis dropped Zora and spun around to face them. "What betrayal is this?"

Grey Cloak started to speak, but Dalsay's commanding voice spoke for him. "This is the end for you, Mortis!" Blue energy shot from the rod like lightning and blasted into Mortis. The searing force sent her down the aisle, and she crashed hard into the door.

Dalsay turned up the heat, sending streams of energy into Mortis's shaking body.

We're doing it! We're doing it! Grey Cloak thought.

Mortis brought her hands in front of her chest and caught the energy in her palms. Then she pushed back and started to march forward.

Grey Cloak's feet slid over the stone floor toward the stage. A wave of energy from Mortis shoved him into the stairs, and he fell. *We're not doing it.*

47

"Fools! I am the queen of this realm. No living person can defeat me!" Mortis said. She slung flaming balls of energy at Grey Cloak. "I am queen!"

Grey Cloak dashed through the rows of pews, ducked a fireball, and sprang away from another. The balls of energy blew out hunks of the pews, and stone dust filled the air.

"Dalsay, I don't know what you're doing, but you need to do better than this."

When Dalsay talked, he spoke in Grey Cloak's head. *"I'm weaving a spell. Keep running."*

Grey Cloak jumped, dove, and rolled then flattened out between the pews and rolled under a stone bench. "How about I hide?" he whispered.

"You run. You hide. You only delay the inevitable!" Mortis said. Stone pews rose from the ground and were tossed aside like hay bales. Stone crashed against stone. The entire chamber was rocked.

Grey Cloak crawled underneath the pews. "Dalsay, how long is this going to take? She's tearing this place to pieces."

The pew he hid under suddenly rose off the ground and was flung aside. It rolled end over end and exploded into a far wall.

He wiggled his fingers at the lich and said, "Oh, hello, Mortis. I love the renovating you're doing. Though I'm not a fan of the Gothic style. But I think it works well with you."

"I can't wait to dry up that tongue of yours," she said as she took a step forward.

The ground beneath her came alive in the form of stone hands and locked onto her legs.

"*Use the rod!*" Dalsay said. "*Use it now!*"

Grey Cloak pointed the tip of the Rod of Weapons at Mortis. "What am I doing?"

"Let go of me!" Mortis demanded. She started breaking out of the stony fingers.

The Rod of Weapons came alive and started firing pulses of mystic blue energy. *Puul-puul-puul-puul-puul.*

The bombs exploded inside the lich's chest. With her legs trapped, she started reeling.

"I like this!" Grey Cloak said. He let out another series of bursts. *Puul-puul-puul-puul-puul.*

Wiry tendrils started to wrap around Mortis's body, pinning her arms to her sides.

"She's trapped!" Grey Cloak hollered. "She's trapped!"

"I can see that. We must act quickly. Sink the rod's spear point into her skull. Hurry!" Dalsay ordered.

"Fools! You cannot kill me! I'm dead everlasting!" Mortis wiggled in her bonds and set her burning eyes on Grey Cloak. "I cannot die!"

"We'll see about that!" Grey Cloak summoned the spear tip's energy and charged.

Fiery beams blasted out of Mortis's eye sockets.

Grey Cloak ducked. "Yipes! I didn't see that coming." He danced away and began an attack from behind.

Mortis's head twisted around. Wherever Grey Cloak went, her eyes followed.

"Dalsay, blind her or something. I can't get close."

"Get as close as you can. I have a better idea," Dalsay replied.

"I will destroy you! I will destroy you all!" Mortis said as she unleashed another fiery blast.

Grey Cloak ducked under the beams and rammed his shoulder into her. Dalsay departed his body and dove into hers.

Grey Cloak's knees wobbled, and he steadied himself with the rod as he clutched his chest. "I feel like my soul was ripped out."

"Strike now!" Dalsay said from inside Mortis's body.

Mortis's eyes had cooled, but they began to burn anew.

Grey Cloak leaped high in the air, summoned the spear

head's energy, and brought the weapon down on the lich's crowned skull. The mystic blast sank down to the black wood.

Mortis's jaw opened wide. "No! You cannot defeat me! You cannot leave this place."

He drove the mystic javelin deeper. "We'll see about that!"

"You will face my wrath!" she screamed. "It will come! I am not the only guard—"

A ring of energy exploded out of Mortis's body and hurled him across the room.

He sat up from a pew with his ears ringing. Dust and debris created a fog in the air. On shaky legs, he walked over to the remains of Mortis. A hole in her skull smoldered. The crown sat cockeyed on her head. A pile of ash and bones and moth-eaten robes lay underneath.

Grey Cloak caught his breath and said, "We did it, Dalsay. Dalsay?"

"What happened?" Zora asked. She was on her feet and rubbing the back of her head. "Who redecorated?"

Jakoby, Leena, and Gorva came to as well. Gorva's leg was deeply cut and bleeding. She walked with a limp. "Where's the wizard?"

"I don't know," Grey Cloak said. His eyes widened. "Dyphestive!" He rushed to the double doors and lifted the locking bar then flung the doors wide open.

Hundreds of zombie soldiers were piled up on the steps

and in the streets. They looked like they had all collapsed under the weight of their armor. The city was dead quiet. There was no sign of Dyphestive.

Grey Cloak cupped his hands over his mouth and shouted, "Dyphestive!"

"The wizard said that we would not all make it out," Gorva said.

"Don't say that!" Zora said.

Jakoby walked over the undead bodies. "Look at the wreckage. Limbs and heads of the zombies are everywhere. Follow the wake of the carnage."

Grey Cloak joined the former Monarch Knight on the stairs and followed the path of destruction. It ended in a pile of zombie soldiers stacked up to Jakoby's neck. "In here!"

Jakoby started dragging the bodies out of the pile. Leena eagerly helped. A limb popped off from time to time, and they chucked them aside.

"They're so brittle," Jakoby said.

Grey Cloak clawed through the dead. He was shoulder deep in the carnage when a gleam of red light caught his eye. "Here! Here!"

With everyone pitching in, they cleared the dead away and found Dyphestive lying on the bottom, covered in his own caked-up blood and not moving.

Grey Cloak pumped his fists in the air and screamed, "Dyphestive!"

48

LEENA PUSHED Grey Cloak aside and held a finger to his lips. She opened Dyphestive's vest and placed both hands over his heart.

"What are you doing?" Grey Cloak asked.

She shook her head and squeezed her eyes shut. Her lips moved quickly, but they made no sound. Strings of white light built up in her shoulder and coursed into her hands. She pushed them into his chest. A shock wave of energy blasted out of her hands.

Dyphestive's body jumped a foot off the ground. He sat up with his eyes wide and said, "Die, zombies! Die!" His arm shot out, and he clamped his hand around Grey Cloak's neck.

Grey Cloak grabbed his brother's wrist and tried to pry

his hand off. Dyphestive's fingers were as strong as iron. "Let go of me," he pleaded in a raspy voice.

Dyphestive blinked a few times, and his grip loosened, then he released Grey Cloak's neck.

Grey Cloak gasped and let out a few dry coughs.

"Sorry," Dyphestive said, patting him on the back. "What happened?"

"You were dead," Gorva said. "The tongueless woman saved you from the Flaming Fence."

Dyphestive raised an eyebrow and said, "I wasn't dead. And I won't ever be crossing the Flaming Fence. I dreamed I was on a cloud, sailing across the sunny sky. And I had an anvil." He pushed out of the pile of the dead and pried a zombie's bony fingers from his ankles. He surveyed the wreckage. "I killed them all?"

"No, you had some help," Gorva said as her gaze slid toward Grey Cloak. "He killed the lich."

"And that killed the rest?" Dyphestive scanned the heaps of the dead and started counting with his finger. "I was up to one hundred twenty-one, and I don't remember anything after that. I blacked out." He picked up his sword. The bloodred gem twinkled like a small star. "Something possessed me."

"One hundred twenty-one?" Jakoby asked as he eyeballed the carnage. "Well, something tore a hole through this one." He lay his hand on Dyphestive's shoulder. "It looks like it was you."

Dyphestive nodded. With his massive hands, he covered Leena's shoulders, looked into her eyes, and he said, "Thank you, but I was only sleeping. But I liked that jolt you gave me." He grinned. "It felt good. Like lightning coursing through my veins."

"So, we can leave?" Zora asked.

Thannis, the city of the dead, had fallen silent. No zombies scuffled or dragged their feet across the street. The rattling and squeaking of armor was gone. The zombies lay in piles like trash in the streets. Even the creeping and crawling spiders were nowhere to be found.

"I believe so," Grey Cloak said as he studied the temple's doors. "But I fear that we lost Dalsay."

"How?" Dyphestive asked. "He was a ghost."

Grey Cloak shook his head. His heart sank into his stomach. He'd thought he didn't care for Dalsay, but now that the wizard was gone, he found that he actually did. "I don't know. But he said certain death awaited. I hope it wasn't his. I'd be responsible."

"You can't kill a ghost," Gorva said. "It's not possible."

"Well, we killed a thousand zombies and a lich, and they were dead." He shrugged. "I don't know." He eyed the temple. "I'm sorry, Dalsay."

Zora hooked his arm. "I'm sure wherever he is, he's fine. But can we go. Not to be selfish, but I don't want to be anywhere near those spiders if they return. We have what we came for, don't we?"

He nodded.

In the distant hills, which were riddled with caves, the clamor of hammers and shovels biting into dirt and stone renewed.

Small bodies crept in an orderly fashion along the shadows of the narrow ledges.

Jakoby squinted and asked, "Who are they?"

"I don't know, and I don't care to find out. Our path is clear, and if there aren't any objections, I say we move out," Grey Cloak said.

"You don't have to tell me twice," Zora said. "Lead the way."

He glanced at Gorva's leg. Leena had started wrapping it with one of her bandages. "Are you well?"

"I can move well enough," Gorva said. She patted Leena on the head. "She's quiet and helpful. I like it."

"Let me know if I move too fast. How about you, Festive?"

Dyphestive glanced over his assortment of wounds. "No troubles."

Grey Cloak led the way down the broken roadways, navigating through the field of the dead. Mortis had boasted that they wouldn't make it out alive, but there they were, living and breathing, with a field of the dead lying at their feet. Not only that, but they'd recovered the Cloak of Legends and the Figurine of Heroes.

I don't know how I did it, but I did. He smirked.

"What are you grinning at?" Zora asked.

"We live. Why wouldn't I be happ—"

The ground rumbled. The buildings rattled and swayed. Ancient shingles slid from rooftops and rained down on the ground.

"Dyphestive," Grey Cloak said, "tell me that was your stomach."

"I'm hungry, but I'm not that hungry."

Grey Cloak looked behind him. The hammering in the hills had come to a stop, and the small figures in the hills had vanished. The tremors tickled his bare feet and sent shivers racing up his spine.

Talon exchanged uncertain glances.

"Friends," Grey Cloak said, "I have an idea."

"We're listening," Gorva said.

A building along the road collapsed like a house of cards. Dust and debris swept down the street. From the smoke, a grand dragon with eyes like purple flames emerged and let out a deafening roar.

Grey Cloak shouted above the clamor, "Run!"

49

"FOLLOW ME!" Grey Cloak hollered. "Follow me!" He'd led them through the twisting streets of Thannis once, and he would have to do it again. He moved them as far away from the sound of the dragon as he could.

They could hear the sounds of buildings crumbling and the dragon's thunderous roar. It went on for several seconds then fell silent.

Grey Cloak ducked into a garden made of massive stones. Gorva held her bloody leg and winced. Everyone was gasping but him.

"Listen, we need to go around the dragon. Get to the entrance to Thannis where we came in."

Zora had her hands on her sides and said, "Maybe it's not even looking for us."

"I wish, but I doubt it. Before Mortis died, she said

something about another guardian. At least I think that's what she was saying. That thing must be it," he said.

"What do you want us to do, Grey?" Dyphestive asked.

"I might have to lead it one way while you go another."

Zora locked her fingers around his wrist and said, "You can't do it all!"

"I agree, brother. We can all get out of here," Dyphestive said. "Whether we kill that thing or die, we stick together."

Grey Cloak nodded. "All right. Everyone, stay close. No one gets separated. We're heading to the field, but if anything happens, be ready to run for your life. We'll only get one chance at this."

The company formed a single-file line and snaked their way deeper into the bowels of the city, heading back toward the fields from where they'd come. Grey Cloak didn't have any trouble picking his way through the wasteland. He could tell where they were by the alignment of the strange lights in the cavern ceiling. The patterns worked like stars, and he remembered them from the moment he'd seen them.

"We are almost to the city's border. It's only two blocks away," he whispered to Zora, who passed the message back to Dyphestive, who guarded the rear.

Grey Cloak peeked down the street. Thannis was walled by stone structures and broken sections of perimeter wall. A wide road led right into the city. There was no sign of the dragon. "I can only imagine the dragon hiding and waiting for us to blow through the main gate." He rubbed his chin. "We need to find a broken section in the wall." He gave Zora the Rod of Weapons. "Hold this and wait here."

His fingers found purchase, and he scaled the wall three stories up to the top of the building. Then he stole across the flat rooftop to a point where he could see over the border wall. "Drat."

They were in a quadrant of the city surrounded by a drop so deep on the other side that he couldn't see a bottom. Staying low, he moved back across the roof and looked over the main road with a full view of the gate. He scanned the streets and alleys.

Where are you, dragon? I know you're out there.

Even though the grand dragon was a tremendous beast, the massive city still had countless places to hide its girth.

As his gaze swept over the storefronts, his heart skipped a beat.

Head down and twisting spiral horns back, the dragon slunk out of the back streets into full view. It was bigger than most. Hard spiny ridges plated its body. Its scales were thick like steel armor. But patches of the scales were missing, revealing rotting flesh and bones underneath.

What kind of undead abomination is that?

Its claws ripped up the street when it passed, and its tail swept over the ground, knocking out the porch posts.

Grey Cloak hurried back to his friends, dropped the last ten feet from the wall, and said to his wide-eyed onlookers, "Change of plans."

"There isn't another way out?" Zora asked.

"We're cornered. Unless we go back into the city and hide, the only way out is through the gate, and as you can see, it has a guardian." He eased his staff out of Zora's hands. "Hence, we are reverting to my first plan."

"No!" Zora said.

"Dyphestive, see to it that you take them to safety. Don't worry about me. If I can lead it away, it won't catch me." He smirked. "I'm too fast."

"We stand together, brother."

"Not this time. Promise me that you will lead all of them out, brother. It is my final request," he said.

Zora's eyes watered. "You can't do this."

"It's like the wizard said—one of us won't make it out," Gorva said. "You are a brave elf. I hope you make it."

Tears streamed down Zora's cheeks. "You'll die out there."

He kissed her on the forehead. "I'll take my chances." Fire blossomed at the end of the Rod of Weapons. He waltzed out into the street and waved it at the undead dragon like a flagon. "Yoo-hoo!"

The guardian dragon swung its head around and set its fiery vermillion gaze on Grey Cloak. It let out a spine-tingling roar. The sound wave ripped off shingles and shutters and blasted through Grey Cloak's hair and cloak.

He pinched his nose and said, "Next time, I'll remember not to breathe." He glanced at his friends hiding in the alley and smirked. Then he faced the dragon, lowered the Rod of Weapons like a lance, and ran straight at the dragon, shouting at the top of his lungs, "Beware the wrath of Grey Cloak!"

50

"HE'S GONE MAD," Zora said.

Dyphestive watched in disbelief as his brother charged the dragon like a berserker and picked up speed. The dragon opened its jaws, revealing a furnace of purple flames.

Grey Cloak planted his feet in the ground, turned, and raced into a narrow alley across the street.

Purple flames carpeted the street a moment after Grey Cloak vanished into the alley. The flames rose high in the air, creating a wall between the buildings.

The heat slapped Dyphestive in the face as if a sweltering blanket had been thrown at him. He pulled Zora back into the alley and shielded her with his body. The heat scorched his back. Everyone in the alley hid their faces and pushed against the wall.

The flames started to die, and Dyphestive looked down the street. The guardian dragon sprinted after Grey Cloak. Its hulking body smashed through the buildings, turning them to rubble. The last of its serpentine tail slipped through the wreckage and vanished.

Stone smashing on stone echoed throughout the once-grand structures of the city. The clamor got farther and farther away.

"Let's go." Dyphestive led the way down the street, where they passed the smoldering flames the dragon had left. A gaping hole made by collapsed buildings twisted through the city.

"Keep moving," Zora said.

Leena shoved the gaping Dyphestive along.

Jakoby followed Gorva, who hurried through the gate with a bad limp.

Dyphestive caught up with them. "Gorva, let us help. We can carry you."

Gorva pulled a dagger and snarled. "If either one of you lays a hand on me, I'll kill you."

Jakoby lifted his hands in surrender. "No problem with me."

"Go, then. Go!" Dyphestive said.

Dragon roars erupted from the street.

He stopped, and Leena shoved him in the back.

"Don't even think about it, Dyphestive," Zora said. "You're staying with us."

Bright flames exploded throughout the city and lit up the tips of the stalactites.

Finally, Dyphestive started moving again.

They raced past the lake, leaped over the fallen undead, and traversed the final hill, where the tunnel to the first inner surface waited. It would be impossible for the guardian dragon to follow them through that tunnel. They had made it to safety.

"We made it," Jakoby said as he hurried Gorva, Zora, and Leena into the tunnel. He eyed Dyphestive. "After you."

Dyphestive shoved Jakoby into the tunnel. "You know I can't leave my brother behind. Get everyone to the surface. We'll meet you there," he said. "I swear it."

Grey Cloak looked over his shoulder and saw the dragon bursting through a building and closing in. "Zooks, that thing is fast!"

Of course, he'd been around his fair share of dragons, and they weren't slow, cumbersome beasts. They were as quick and agile as little lizards in some cases. But the undead one was bones and scales. He'd hoped it would move more slowly, but it didn't.

He jumped through a tavern window and raced up a

flight of steps. The dragon crashed through the door below and unleashed its fiery breath. The flames incinerated the steps and raced down the hall after Grey Cloak. He jumped through the window at the other end and landed as softly as a cat in the street.

Flames consumed the building, and the guardian dragon smashed through the back wall, set its eyes on Grey Cloak, and roared.

"Flaming fences!" He channeled his energy into his feet and took off down the street at full speed. With the Cloak of Legends as his companion, he'd become confident that his plan would work. He would run the dragon ragged, buying time for his friends to escape. Once he thought a reasonable enough amount of time had cleared, he would run after them. There was no way the guardian dragon could follow them into the tunnels. It was far too large to do so.

He hurdled fallen zombies and took every narrow street he could find. The dragon plowed through everything like a juggernaut while spitting balls of flame at him.

I can't shake this thing!

The dragon didn't have to see him. Once it had his scent, it could follow him blind if it wanted.

Grey Cloak ran to the far end of the city and entered Mortis's temple. He slammed the metal doors behind him. His lungs burned—and his lungs *never* burned.

He ran to the stage then turned and ran back toward the doors, stole his way along the front entrance wall, and hid behind the pillars.

The dragon rammed through the heavy metal doors like they were made of glass. It pushed its great girth into the building, squeezing through the opening. Pews were pulverized as it passed, and it crushed the crown and the remains of Mortis under its feet. It approached the stage, letting out loud snorts through its nose, and released a geyser of flame.

Grey Cloak dashed away from his hiding spot and squirted out the front entrance of the building. He hit the steps running at full speed and ran over the undead.

He'd made it several blocks down the road when he heard the temple explode and glanced over his shoulder. The entire temple was an inferno. The guardian dragon crept out and roared.

My plan's working. It won't catch me now!

He ran even faster. The wind whistled by his ears like an arrow.

Zooks, how fast am I going?

It had happened once before, long ago, when the Cloak of Legends spurred him to incredible speeds that defied reason.

Grey Cloak cleared the main city gate like a shot. Far behind him, the dragon steamrolled after him. The only things between him and freedom were the hills and the glassy surface of the lake.

He smirked. *It would be quicker if I didn't have to go around the lake. Can I? Will I? I have to try!*

Grey Cloak went down the grassy bank, and when his toes touched water, he kept going.

I'm doing it! I can't believe I'm doing it!

He had run over the cool surface halfway when he caught someone waving out of the corner of his eye. Dyphestive stood on the side of the lake, flagging him down.

"No, Dyphestive, what are you doing? Go the other way!" He skidded over the water and started to sink.

The guardian dragon charged through the gate of the flaming city.

"Run, Dyphestive! Run!"

The dragon didn't see Grey Cloak and set its sights on Dyphestive.

Grey Cloak swam for the bank. He reached the edge and climbed up.

Dyphestive stood his ground and faced the dragon with the iron sword in hand.

"No!" Grey Cloak ran to his brother's aid, but he wouldn't get there in time.

Dyphestive lunged forward and thrust hard. Brawn and metal collided with dragon skull and scales. The bloodred gem in the cross guard flashed.

The guardian dragon came to a stop. It trembled and roared. The iron sword pierced its skull between the eyes. It twisted the sword free from Dyphestive's grip and bucked like a mule. Dyphestive backed away.

It burned from the inside out. Scale and bone caught fire. The monster exploded, hurling chunks of bone and scale everywhere.

The guardian dragon lay in a smoldering pile. The light in its eyes was gone. The flame inside it had been snuffed out.

Dyphestive pulled his sword free of the mammoth skull.

"You killed it," Grey Cloak said as he shook the water from his cloak. "I'm not sure how you did it, but well done."

Dyphestive's gaze ran along his blade to the gemstone, which had cooled. "I don't know how it happened either." He smiled. "But what's done is done. We did it."

"Let's get out of here," Grey Cloak said. "I've had my fill of dead people."

They navigated through the tunnels without any trouble and passed through the field of glowing dandelions into the last tunnel, which took them to the Inland Sea's waterfall.

"I can't wait to see the sun again," Dyphestive said, "and eat like a Monarch."

Grey Cloak nodded. "I share your sentiments. A feast is in order. Now that I have the figurine and the cloak and you have a fine sword, hopefully, we can get the world back in order."

"Agreed." Dyphestive was the first to stick his head out of the tunnel, and the mist of the river kissed his face. He stood on the ledge with the sun shining on the other side of the water and washed the blood from his skin.

Grey Cloak frowned. His brother was torn up all over from at least a dozen lacerations and wounds. He didn't understand how he'd made it. He gestured to the rope and said, "After you."

"Let's go at the same time and surprise our friends together."

Grey Cloak smiled. "I like surprises. I bet they're sleeping. I know I would be after all that adventure."

Dyphestive climbed the rope.

Grey Cloak used the small handholds in the face of the cliff.

Side by side, brother and brother, they scaled the sheer wall. Before they crested the top, they grinned at one another and counted in silence. "One... two... three..."

They climbed over the lip, jumped up, and shouted, "Surprise!"

Grey Cloak felt the blood run out of him.

Dyphestive's mouth hung open.

They stood face-to-face with Drysis the Dreadful and the Doom Riders.

"Surprise indeed," Drysis said with her crossbow

pointed at Grey Cloak's chest. "Welcome back to the land of the living—well, except for me."

What do the Doom Riders have in store for the blood brothers?

Can Tatiana stop the underlings before they master the Time Mural?

Where is Black Frost in all of this?

Grab Book 11 – Death in the Desert – on sale now!

And don't forget, please leave a review of PERIL IN THE DARK - BOOK 10 when you finish. I've typed my fingers to the bone writing it and your reviews are a huge help!

PERIL IN THE DARK REVIEW LINK

Buy Death in the Desert now!

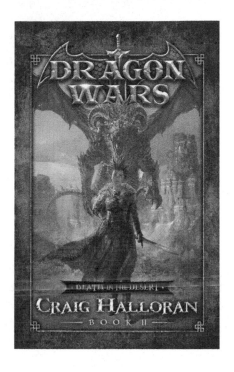

And if you haven't already, signup for my newsletter and grab 3 FREE books including the Dragon Wars Prequel.

WWW.DRAGONWARSBOOKS.COM

Teachers and Students, if you would like to order paperback copies for you library or classroom, email craig@thedarkslayer.com to receive a special discount.

Gear up in this Dragon Wars body armor enchanted with a +2 Coolness factor/+4 at Gaming Conventions. Sizes range from halfling (Small) to Ogre (XXL). LINK . www.society6.com

ABOUT THE AUTHOR

Craig Halloran resides with his family outside his hometown of Charleston, West Virginia. When he isn't entertaining mankind, he is seeking adventure, working out, or watching sports. To learn more about him, go to WWW.-DRAGONWARSBOOKS.COM.

*Check me out on Bookbub and follow: HalloranOn-BookBub

*I'd love it if you would subscribe to my mailing list: www.craighalloran.com

*On Facebook, you can find me at The Darkslayer Report or Craig Halloran.

*Twitter, Twitter, Twitter. I am there, too: www.twitter.com/CraigHalloran

*And of course, you can always email me at craig@thedarkslayer.com

See my book lists below!

ALSO BY CRAIG HALLORAN

OTHER BOOKS

Craig Halloran resides with his family outside his hometown of Charleston, West Virginia. When he isn't entertaining mankind, he is seeking adventure, working out, or watching sports. To learn more about him, go to www.thedarkslayer.com.

The Chronicles of Dragon Series 1 (10-book series)

The Hero, the Sword and the Dragons (Book 1)

Dragon Bones and Tombstones (Book 2)

Terror at the Temple (Book 3)

Clutch of the Cleric (Book 4)

Hunt for the Hero (Book 5)

Siege at the Settlements (Book 6)

Strife in the Sky (Book 7)

Fight and the Fury (Book 8)

War in the Winds (Book 9)

Finale (Book 10)

Boxset 1-5

Boxset 6-10

Collector's Edition 1-10

Tail of the Dragon, The Chronicles of Dragon, Series 2 (10-book series)

Tail of the Dragon #1

Claws of the Dragon #2

Battle of the Dragon #3

Eyes of the Dragon #4

Flight of the Dragon #5

Trial of the Dragon #6

Judgement of the Dragon #7

Wrath of the Dragon #8

Power of the Dragon #9

Hour of the Dragon #10

Boxset 1-5

Boxset 6-10

Collector's Edition 1-10

The Odyssey of Nath Dragon Series (New Series) (Prequel to Chronicles of Dragon)

Exiled

Enslaved

Deadly

Hunted

Strife

The Darkslayer Series 1 (6-book series)

Wrath of the Royals (Book 1)

Blades in the Night (Book 2)

Underling Revenge (Book 3)

Danger and the Druid (Book 4)

Outrage in the Outlands (Book 5)

Chaos at the Castle (Book 6)

Boxset 1-3

Boxset 4-6

Omnibus 1-6

The Darkslayer: Bish and Bone, Series 2 (10-book series)

Bish and Bone (Book 1)

Black Blood (Book 2)

Red Death (Book 3)

Lethal Liaisons (Book 4)

Torment and Terror (Book 5)

Brigands and Badlands (Book 6)

War in the Wasteland (Book 7)

Slaughter in the Streets (Book 8)

Hunt of the Beast (Book 9)

The Battle for Bone (Book 10)

Boxset 1-5

Boxset 6-10

Bish and Bone Omnibus (Books 1-10)

CLASH OF HEROES: Nath Dragon meets The Darkslayer mini series

Book 1

Book 2

Book 3

The Henchmen Chronicles

The King's Henchmen

The King's Assassin

The King's Prisoner

The King's Conjurer

The King's Enemies

The King's Spies

The Gamma Earth Cycle

Escape from the Dominion

Flight from the Dominion

Prison of the Dominion

The Supernatural Bounty Hunter Files (10-book series)

Smoke Rising: Book 1

I Smell Smoke: Book 2

Zombie Impact Series

OTHER WORKS & NOVELLAS

The Red Citadel and the Sorcerer's Power

Made in the USA
Monee, IL
23 May 2021